ALSO BY CYNTHIA D. BERTELSEN

MUSHROOM: A Global History

A HASTINESS OF COOKS:
A Practical Handbook for Use in Deciphering the Mysteries of
Historic Recipes and Cookbooks

IN THE SHADOW OF RAVENS: A Novel

WISDOM SOAKED IN PALM OIL:
Journeying Through the Food and Flavors of Africa

MEATBALLS & LEFSE:
Memories and Recipes from a
Scandinavian-American Farming Life

STOVES & SUITCASES:
Searching for Home in the World's Kitchens

TAKE A GOOSE OR A DUCK:
Eclectic Essays on English Cookery Through the Ages

MANGOES & ROOSTERS

STORIES AND TALES OF HAITI

Cynthia D. Bertelsen

TURQUOISE
MOON PRESS

Mangoes & Roosters
Stories and Tales of Haiti

This is a work of fiction. Aside from the "The Dictator," the characters here represent no person, either living or dead.

Haitian proverbs from *Hidden Meanings* by Wally Turnbull
©torchflamebooks.com.
Used with permission.

Cover image: Cover background: AdobeStock – 345047537
Cover and book design: Cathy Gibbons Reedy
ISBN: 978-1-7345579-4-7
Library of Congress Control Number: 2022913569

Turquoise Moon Press
Gainesville, FL

TURQUOISEMOONPRESS.COM

For my father,
Laurence Henry Purdy
(1926-2015)

I miss you every day.

The following fictional stories reflect those of the many characters and archetypes who populated Haiti in the past and continue to do so in the present, as well as the devastating earthquake of January 12, 2010.

Lè w lan peyi blan ou pa wè mango ni kòk di tou
Lanpwen sapoti ni bèl kayimit vèt ou vyolèt
Lanpwen zanana ni bèl ti pòm kajou
Ki ban nou bon nwa pou nou fè bon ti tablèt

When you're in the White man's country, you don't see
mangoes or roosters anywhere,
Not sapoti or beautiful green and purple star apples,
No pineapples or beautiful cashew apples,
Those that give us great cashews for delicious brittle.

~ Othello Bayard, "Haiti Cherie," 1925

TABLE OF CONTENTS

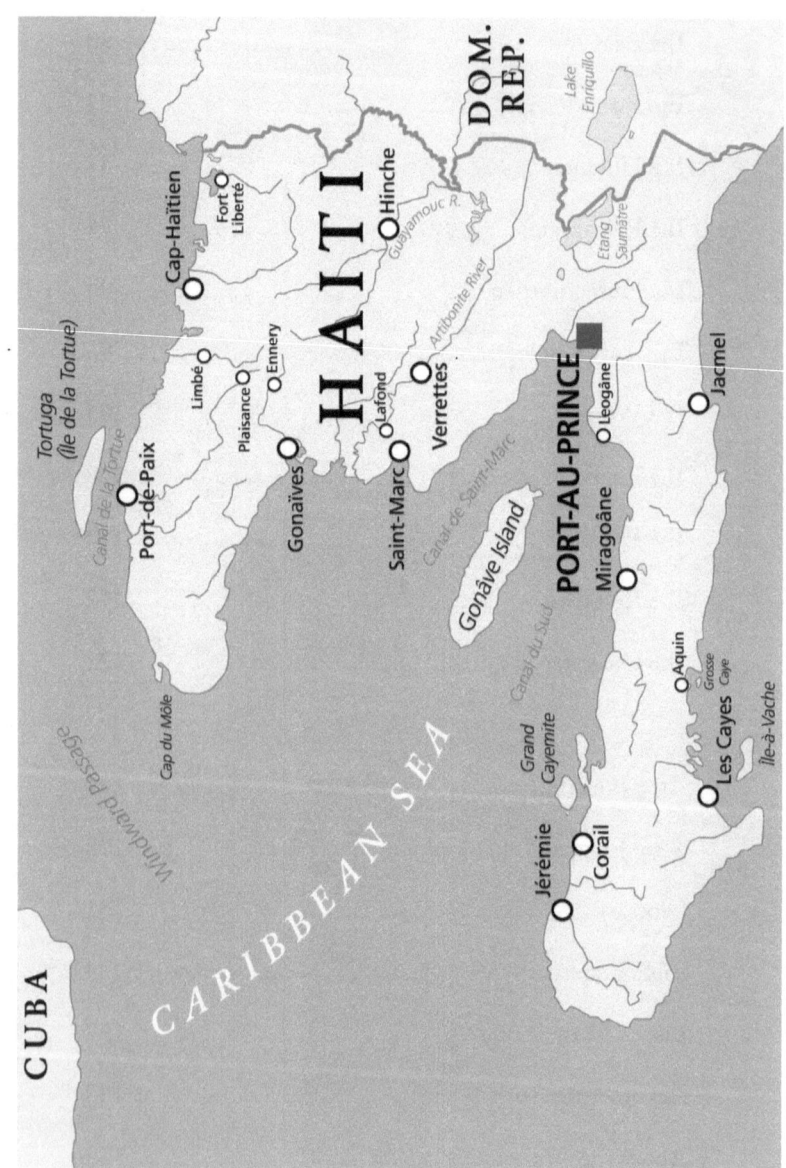

PROLOGUE

Smoke never rises without fire.
~ Haitian proverb

I SUPPOSE I'VE ALWAYS HAD A YEN for the unusual, the bizarre, the edge-of-the-knife experience. When word came that a job in Haiti turned up, out of the blue, one cold day in northern New York state, why, there was no question of not going. My life at the time consisted of long days at a worn writing table, pecking away at the yellow Smith-Corona typewriter, a relic from my college years, seeking to place meaning on thin sheets of 16-weight paper without tearing the delicate matrix.

At the time, all I knew about Haiti I'd learned from Graham Greene's morality tale, *The Comedians*. Banned in Haiti, now a dog-eared Penguin version buried between half a dozen Caribbean cookbooks in my luggage. You see, Papa Doc Duvalier took Greene's words personally and even wrote a pamphlet attacking Greene's moral turpitude, labeling him with every degenerate trait imaginable. "Graham Greene *Demasqué*." I smuggled in *The Comedians* to remind myself of what I was getting into once I boarded the plane in Miami for the hour-and-a-half flight to Port-au-Prince.

Port-au-Prince, I could see it from the vantage point of the tiny airplane window, the crescent shape of the Bay of Gonâve outlining the contours of the sprawling city, curved like a child sleeping in its cradle. Although I'd traveled widely throughout the Caribbean and Central

America, those experiences failed to prepare me for the blast of heat and moisture-soaked air, the fumes of burnt charcoal hanging in the air. I hesitated for a moment at the top of the stairway leading to the tarmac below, watching the crowd milling about on the other side of the rickety wire fence. Nudged by the person behind me, I started down the steps, noticing four men swathed in dark blue denim, aviator sunglasses glinting in the noonday sun, rifles slung over rippling shoulders.

Tontons Macoutes!

They paid no attention to me, but a loud scream behind me acted as a signal. As one, the men grabbed the stairway railing and plunged upward, knocking me to the side. I raced down the steps and ran toward the terminal. Then, fool-heartedly, I stood and watched, wondering what might happen next. In seconds, down they came again, a weeping man gripped on either side, dragging him by his arms across the smoldering tarmac to a Jeep spewing dark oily smoke from its rusty tailpipe.

I walked through the smudged glass doors of the airport, expecting a blast of cool air. If anything, the inside air blistered my lungs, hotter than that outside. I glanced behind me. The weeping, blubbering man disappeared into the Jeep as the Macoutes swung into the back of the Jeep, pounding the man with their rifle butts, over and over again.

I thought then of my copy of *The Comedians*. Praying that an illiterate customs official would not see Greene's name on the smuggled book, so engrossed he would be by the colorful photographs on the cookbook covers. Hopefully, he would wink at me and, with a wave of his hand, drone, *"Bienvenue à Haiti,"* tugging at the collar of his frayed airline uniform.

"Welcome to Haiti."

And to tragedy, not comedy.

ॐॐ

THE MACOUTE

The rat that has only one hole dies easily.
~ Haitian proverb

THE MIRROR REFLECTED ALL THE THINGS he hated about his face.

The crooked nose, witness to his father's rage one June night, too much clairin fogging his reason.

The bald spot, where he'd scraped the skin down to the bone when the five Laguerre brothers ambushed him in the alley and stole the eggs he carried, meant for the market.

The missing front teeth, a souvenir of yet another encounter, that time with the priest, Father Baptiste, no true believer of Jesus, no, not that devil.

He sighed. Picking up the rough denim shirt, he pulled it over his thick biceps and buttoned it, to the next to last button, leaving tufts of curling black hair poking out. Then the gold chains, all four of them, of varying thicknesses, draped around his neck, glittering snakes worthy of King Midas's counting house.

Lastly, the belt, with hidden pockets for bullets, crafted from the tanned leather of unfortunate cattle. The bush hat, denim as well. Red scarf, the color of blood.

But the thing he cherished most was the sunglasses. A pilot's sunglasses. With mirror-like lenses. Wrongdoers could see their terrified faces as he brandished his machete close to their eyes, their noses, with an occasional quick slash of a cheek, exposing teeth and tongues.

Last, the rifle, rusty and temperamental as it was,

cradled in his arms, recalling the feeling of holding a new-born child.

He didn't wear it, but he tucked it into his mind every bit as much as he tucked his shirt under his belt.

Fear.

And fear was power to him. He might be unable to read or write, at least nothing more than his name, maybe his face was ugly, but he could instill fear. He grinned.

Turning away from the mirror, he took a few steps across the room. His wife shrank back when he thrust out his hand, touching their infant son's head, who lay swaddled from head to toe in her thin arms. He walked out the door into the sunshine, watching with satisfaction as the neighbors scurried away like cockroaches under his shining gaze.

He swaggered down the road, dodging muddy potholes, swinging the rifle in his left hand, his right poised over the nightstick at his waist. The air felt fresh from the night's rain. When he came to the corner, he heard the radio blaring from the lean-to of the clairin seller. And caught everyone glaring at him, eyes wide open, mouths set and grim.

A voice on the radio droned in the background. The dictator's son was gone, flying to France at that very moment. *Haiti libre*!

The drumming of his heart throbbed in his ears and chest, in unison with the drums tapping out the message of freedom. He was no longer free. He sensed that in the deepest recesses of his brain. Before he could run, back to his house, his wife, his son, hands grabbed him, punching him, breaking his nose once again, shattering the gleaming glasses. In the shards, he saw his own face, his fear as he stared at the ground. Other hands stripped him until he stood as naked as the day God called him to earth.

Oh no, not the necklace, not that! Shoot me, club me. But don't do that.

On went the old tire that'd lain on the ground at the crossroads ever since he could remember. Around his neck. The pungent fumes of the gasoline kept him from fainting despite his bleeding, damaged nose. Chanting, the crowd shoved him to the ground. The flicker of a cigarette lighter hissed near his ear.

Moaning, tears streaming his eyes, pinking the blood, he watched the grinning faces surrounding him as the gasoline caught fire, rubber melting.

I'm sorry, I'm sorry!

৵৹৻

THE DICTATOR

Exile is better than being shot.
~ Haitian proverb

Nothing much haunted him. That was true.

He could go to Fort Dimanche and watch the slow torture of one of his enemies with the exact same pleasure he got when playing polo with his rich English friends or drinking rum on his million-dollar yacht with the sons of the Haitian elite. They called him "Basket Head" behind his back, secure in the knowledge that no one, not even he, could touch them.

Or so they believed.

Maybe not through the usual arrest-and-torture route, no.

But their wallets were much thinner when I got through with them.

He chuckled quietly at the memories. His fingers reached far, in banks and in other ways. Some would say tentacles as thick as those of octopuses swimming in the Bay of Gonâve.

From his window on the U.S. Air Force plane, he gazed at the lights of Port-au-Prince below. His wife sat across from him, the white turban she'd worn on the way to the airport now tossed into a puddle-like rumpled pile of purses, carry-ons, and a cold bottle of Veuve-Clicquot. He shook his head when the steward offered a tulip-shaped glass of the champagne.

How did this happen? Why didn't the people love me?

They loved my father. Didn't they? Didn't they???

Even the Tontons Macoutes failed him. When the heat on the street began to scorch them, they turned tail and ran, dropping their denim shirts and pants and mirror-lens sunglasses in their wake. The ignorant masses believed the Macoutes embodied the *loa* Kouzin Zaka, a being similar to the boogeyman of childhood dreams around the world. They also revered his father as Baron Samedi, the Lord of the Cemetery, one of the *loa* associated with death. Maybe, just maybe, the man himself imagined it to be the truth as well.

He shuddered at the thought of his father, garbed in black, the suit of a man headed to the grave, with a shiny, black top hat crowning the ensemble. He beckoned to the steward. His wife and children sat across the aisle, oblivious to his musings. As the steward handed him another flute of bubbling champagne, he filched yet another, drinking both as if they held water and not one of France's most prestigious wines.

On the bright side, I'm going to live in France.

Revived by the wine, he stood and stretched. He walked through the curtain separating him from the rest of the plane, nodding to those in his entourage as he went. Who didn't want to "wait and see" what would happen when he no longer wielded power. He ignored the *blans*, mostly NGO and USAID workers evacuated from the countryside.

Like rats fleeing the sinking ship.

Dulled by the champagne, he sank back into his seat, which generals and admirals used on routine flights back to the U.S. Eyes closed, the rumble of the plane lulled him into a twilight sleep. He mumbled a prayer to the *loa*, imagining the plane's drone to be drumming, a sound incessant in the hills and mountains of Haiti over the last three months.

With a flash, as though a lightning bolt crisscrossed his brain, his being cleaved in two.

Somewhere, somehow, someone with power was calling him back, back to Haiti, back to a place where he only had to say, "Do it!" And whatever that was, it was done.

But he seemed to be falling, cartwheeling through the air, landing hard on the seat of his limo, his driver leering at him, the car going nowhere.

Drive, drive. Faster, go faster, you dolt!

Still no movement. Against the glass of the automobile, face after face pressed close. Bloodied faces, tongueless mouths, eyeless heads with no eyes, limbless torsos. Like a drowning man, he struggled to reach a place of clear air. He looked away. Fingers pointed at him, hands outstretched, the car rocked with waves of anger, decades of hurt and loss and starvation, sounds of howling and lament. In this terrifying whirlpool of damaged humanity, he raised his face to the window again.

A man struggled through the crowd, coming toward him, a flaming tire around his neck, his glowing skin melting, eyes wide and white and wild, mouth split with a silent cry. He shrank back as the man pressed his face against the glass. There he saw the face of his dear childhood friend, suffering the Haitian equivalent of the Crucifixion. Paying for sins, transgressions, all committed in his father's name, then his own. Necklacing, they called it.

Hands shook him awake, his screaming echoing throughout the plane.

It was just a dream, just a dream!!

But no.

In the days and years to come, the world would learn of the evil below the surface in Haiti.

It was just a dream, just a dream!!

The sins of the fathers ....

ॐॐ

THE COOK

The fish's mouth gets him hooked.
~ Haitian proverb

She moved with the sleek grace of a black cat slipping through jungle darkness, silent, unobtrusive, knowing. The guests barely noticed when she set the plates of fried pork and *djon-djon* rice in front of them, her actions only perceptible through a slight shift in the air as she moved to the next person at the long wooden table. Outside, past the slatted shutters, rain fell the way rain always falls in the tropics, hard, fast, Noah's ark-like.

She once cooked for the dictator, and some people insisted she was a spy, a snitch as it went in prison jargon. Gossip thrives whenever, wherever two people meet. As she recalled those days, she turned and peered closely at the man at the end of the expansive, wooden table. Her dark eyes bore into his with the intensity of a leopard stalking its prey. His familiar grey-flecked goatee distinguished him from the other seven men.

Holy Jesus, can he read my mind?

He pointed at the French baguette, apparently oblivious to who she was. She nodded, then disappeared into the kitchen, through swinging doors that would be right at home in one of Italian director Sergio Leone's spaghetti western films.

The man's presence seemed to fill the dining room, even following her into the kitchen. She shivered as she reached for the bread, slicing it with the dull, rusty knife she'd bought at the Iron Market. When she squinted at the doors, she still sensed that goatee bobbing up and down as the man talked and chewed. Her inattention to the knife caused her to nick her left index finger. Blood spurted and dripped down her arm when she raised it, grabbing a rag to staunch the crimson flood.

Is he here to drag me back to that devil's den?

The bleeding controlled, she finished cutting the rest of the baguette and stacked the pieces in a basket lined with a clean, white kitchen towel.

All the guests went silent when she burst through the doors. The man smiled at her, while the rest of the diners slurped their water or wine.

She set the bread down with a quick flick of her wrist, but she wasn't fast enough. The man gripped her by the elbow. Startled by the strength of his long, well-manicured fingers, and lulled by his soft voice and the aroma of cigar smoke, she leaned forward as he whispered, his mustache tickling her cheek, so close were they.

Jerking her arm from his grasp, she wanted nothing more than to leave, escaping through the flapping doors and into the deluging rain. To be cleansed, to forget her sin.

As she stood at the kitchen door, she turned, staring at the man, who mouthed that terrible word at her again: *Murderer.*

Because the rest of the guests returned to their meal, once in the kitchen, alone, she sighed with a tinge of relief. She knew she'd never cook again in this house, a place where she'd finally felt safe, sure never to cross paths with any of those old Macoutes surrounding the dictator. The men who'd dragged her from the kitchen in the palace, left her to rot in Dessalines prison.

For poisoning the dictator. Attempting to, rather.

Two days later, after beatings and sleep deprivation, she'd been released, welcomed back at the palace, a prodigal daughter. The real culprit bragged of his deed in the wrong place, the gossip reached the ears of the dictator, and the bigmouthed man died before he could tell the whole story.

That year the foxglove grew as fast as bamboo all over the island. Or so it seemed.

And my foxglove galloped across my garden, too.

The Maid

Greater takes a bigger fall.
~ Haitian proverb

RAIN IN LABOULE FELL LIKE STONES thrown by an angry god. It tore through the barren, jagged Haitian mountains, yet at the same time caressing the earth with dense gray fog, dense as the smoke of the countless cooking fires lit at the first sign of the morning sun. The three dogs sniffed her feet as she yawned, pulling at her short curly hair adorned with a threadbare red scarf, the color of blood and the flowers of the flamboyant tree. Of the Haitian flag, too.

Go away!

She mumbled to the female dog licking her big toe.

Don't bother me!

She slapped at the dog's bony head. The dog slunk away, muted growling tumbling from its scrawny throat. It wasn't that she didn't like the dogs. No, they were her friends, they barked at night and during the day when she was alone in the big house on the ridge. They kept her safe, although the gardener would never try anything untoward. The Wackenhut security guards might, as they lounged in their black Suburban, smoking, laughing, playing the radio, blaring rap music. That is until the missus complained to the bosses the noise kept her awake all night. Still, drums and gunfire from down the mountain echoed in the darkness, every night.

Sometimes she stood on the second-floor balcony.

Wondering what it would be like to be the missus. Wondering what life might be with an American passport and the power it wielded.

But she needed to get upstairs and start her day's chores. Cleaning the bathrooms, sweeping the floors, feeding the three dogs, washing the dishes.

On the stairs leading up to the house, she saw it.

Red rivulets seeped wetly down each step, as though someone'd been painting and hadn't cleaned up the dribbles. The dogs sniffed at the blood, and the head, nearly severed from the body. Every hair on her scalp tingled, and she threw her hand over her mouth, stopping the silent scream about to break the quiet of the morning. She knew what that broken, bloodied carcass meant. It was for her, not the American family. She couldn't tell them that the man who owned their house was a houngan and not the white magic type either. No, he shared the same mind, one as menacing as the Macoutes who watched her when she stepped off the tap-tap at the foot of the mountain.

All because of another man, the one who controlled her every thought.

Thinking of him raised the hair on the back of her neck. Almost as straight as the razor he always threatened her with.

But what can I do? Her father murdered his father for raping her mother. I may even be his sister. Please, Erzulie, not that!

For what he did to her behind the curtain, away from the eyes of her three children, well, she suspected that God himself would never forgive it.

And by merely thinking of him, he appeared, stepping out from the laundry room behind her. Clasping his hand over her mouth, he snarled at her.

Get the money you're always talking about. The money the blans keep inside that book.

He shoved her toward the steps up to the house's kitchen.

A noise, a door slamming.

She stiffened.

Madam! No, she's in the kitchen.

But he pushed her harder, and she stumbled over the dead carcass.

At the kitchen door, he sidled up to the wall so he wouldn't be seen. She pushed open the door, her head shaking as if a strong wind blew over her. She forced herself to smile at Madam and mumbled something about cleaning upstairs.

The book, the book, which one was it?

She scrambled through the pages with her quivering hands. Then she heard the yelling below.

Her heart thumped in her chest, as powerful a sound in her ears as thunder rolling over the barren mountains on a blustery hurricane day.

Downstairs, Madam stood at the doorway, berating him, warning him never to come back again. He resembled a cornered wild boar, teeth exposed, hands digging into his pockets. When the gardener pulled open the gate, the rasping sound startled him. The man turned, knocking into the gardener as he bolted, feet pounding the muddy red road leading to Petionville.

She waited, her breath coming in short gasps, her brain fogging from the lack of air. Madam turned to her, blue eyes blazing with the sheen of opals, and said the words she hoped not to hear.

Done, pack up, and leave.

She dropped to her knees, sobbing.

No, no, no! No, Madam, you don't know what he'll do to me if I come back empty-handed.

Madam pointed to the door. With tears streaming down her cheeks, she gripped Madam around the knees, so tightly that Madam and the gardener used all their force to pry her off.

All she could think of as she walked slowly down the mountain was that gleaming razor.

≈∞≈

THE GARDENER

Remember the rain that sprouts your corn.
~ Haitian proverb

HE STOOD IN THE DUSTY ROAD, outside the gate, his rumpled, sweat-stained bush hat askew on his graying hair, his sinewy arms reaching toward the single white cotton ball-shaped cloud. Chanting filled the air, echoing through the valley, seemingly bouncing off the limestone rocks jutting from the thin, red topsoil.

If the skies didn't fill with rain soon, if the gods failed to bless him this year, his meager crops struggling on the ridge across the valley would wither and die. And his family would starve, despite the generous salary he garnered from his gardening job with the *blans*. He swayed with the soft gusts whipping up the dust, moving faster and faster as the wind picked up speed.

As he swirled in the tiny cyclones of soil, the dogs began to howl, especially the sandy-colored bitch with eyes lined with black hairs, as if someone took kohl and painted her lids. The black one who ate her puppies sidled up to him, sniffing at his bare feet. He kicked her, and she squealed, running off to hide under the Jeep parked in the driveway of the big house. She convulsed with fear as the first thunderclap shook the terracotta tiles of the house's roof and burrowed down behind one of the tires. The *blans* made him bathe those mutts, so he tied them to the sterile papaya tree at the back of the house. There he hosed them down with chilly water and lathered them until they looked as white as the *blans*.

The dizziness produced by his dancing brought the god Damballah to him, as the god owned him. He began whistling, dropped to the ground, slithering now across the dirt in the manner of the serpent god. People passing on the road witnessed his dance, his chanting. A few *Madan Saras* placed eggs and cornmeal in his wake, while one toddling child reached into a burlap sack and placed a small plastic bag of white rice in the road as well.

The dogs wailed in earnest as a crowd surrounded him, clapping, throwing their heads back, chanting, "Damballah, Damballah!"

Dark clouds gathered over Kenscoff, and milk-white fog rolled down the valley, carpeting the denuded hillsides. Lightning struck the bare earth, so empty of plant life that no strike set anything afire.

Raindrops fell faster and faster, splattering the soil so hard that small craters formed, like the aftermath of small bombs falling. Most of the people on the road scattered, racing toward home. Others stood still, gleefully bathing in the deluge, grateful after months of drought.

The feel of cool water on his dusty skin brought him out of the trance. He stood, gathered the offerings and placed them in the crook of his elbow. The dogs lay under the Jeep, quivering with each boom of thunder. Even the *blans* emerged from the French doors onto the patio at the back of the house, where they opened their mouths and drank the drops. Like nectar, too. The cistern filling, the crops drinking, the people singing.

As he walked home, he remembered what the old man told him, his grandfather, about corn and rain.

The Guard

He gave him a cigarette lit at both ends.
~ Haitian proverb

THE *blans* FINALLY DIMMED THEIR LIGHTS as the dogs snuffled nearby, tails wrapped close to their plump, muscular bodies. He looked longingly at the large stainless-steel dish, a few bites of cornmeal mush and bits of beef drying in the crisp air. Madam cooked for the dogs. Making mush from prime cornmeal and beef bones she bought from the French butcher on the corner of the square in Petionville. Food he could only afford on saints' days or Christmas. His stomach rumbled. He reached into the bowl with his fingers, digging into the cold mass. Cupping his hand around a baseball-size blob of *mouli*, he stuck it in his mouth, licking his scarred fingers. His stomach quieted for a moment. The sounds of the evening became more evident in the quietness.

He thought for a moment about the night five Tontons dragged his father off to Fort Dimanche, for stealing a chicken to feed his brothers and sisters. He'd dared to interfere, his reward the butt-end of a rifle on his hand, shattering two fingers and nearly severing another.

Sitting on the hard wooden chair, he yearned for a cigarette. The smoke kept Madam awake, so he split open a Comme il Faut and chewed the raw, bitter tobacco. His eyes felt heavy, but his brain moved with the speed of a runaway mule. What was that story the crazy gardener told him, about the dead carcass on the steps that morning, moments before Madam fired the maid? That was no loss to him, the bitch constantly teased him with her swaying hips and mouthy words. But that guy, her husband, her boyfriend, whatever he was, *he* needed to be gone.

He rubbed his eyes.

I can't see! Why can't I see?

Out in the darkness, a translucent figure loomed, coming straight at him. Hovering over him, the apparition gripped him by the throat, and a half-birthed whimper faded like a tropical sunset, quick, gone in the time it took to blink. Then, in the dimness of his mind, he remembered.

The cigarette!

He'd pilfered it from the maid's room after she ran weeping from the sight of the gory carcass.

Why did she have cigarettes? She didn't smoke!

The dogs woke at the sound of his muffled cries. They yipped, delighted at his jerky movements. The more he danced in the arms of the specter, the more excited they became. Jumping up on him, nipping at his toes poking out from the worn plastic flip-flops.

Aargh! Aargh!

His muffled yells brought no one to his aid. He collapsed on the ground in front of the kitchen door, his head resting against the bumper of Madam's Subaru.

He shut his eyes, tight. When he opened one, fearful of what he might see, the specter evaporated into the darkness. Then the kitchen door sprang open with such force that he trembled, fearing the wraith's return.

Madam stood there, a kitchen knife gleaming in her hand, her hair whipping around her face, reminiscent of a nest of hissing snakes.

He screamed, drawing his legs to his chest, the position of a newborn child. The dogs licked his face. Madam closed the door, and the darkness returned.

But he didn't go back to his chair. Instead, he threw the rest of the cigarette into the toilet in the maid's room and flushed it. He opened the gate and sprinted down the rutted road, the dogs chasing him in their playful delusion.

I quit. I quit.

The next night, he slunk over the ridge to see who the *blans* hired in his place, after he told the gardener he'd never go back, to tell Madam sorry, but no. Surprised, he saw the Wackenhut truck roll up to the gate, with four beefy men dressed in spiffy uniforms, Macoutes by day. The guns on their hips banging against their thighs with a clack-clack. All four smoking. Right under Madam's bedroom window.

He smiled.

Au revoir, he mouthed and pivoted toward the road.

৯৩•৯৩

THE MADAN SARA

Hunger in the stomach isn't sweet.
~ Haitian proverb

THE NEEDLES AND PINS FEELING IN HER BREASTS stopped her in the middle of the street. Balancing the basket on her head, she reached up and, with both hands, settled it on the ground in front of her. Then she grabbed her paisley head cloth and pressed it against her chest. She was a big woman, and she'd be compared to certain linebackers in places far away.

Having stifled the flow of milk, she forced herself to stop thinking of her baby at home, home being a shack cobbled together with pieces of torn moldy cardboard and scrounged sheet metal from abandoned construction sites, best entered at night under the shine of a full moon.

She bent over, lifted the basket, and placed it on her head once again. Almost the width of a truck tire, the basket weighed heavily on her neck, so much so that she could barely sleep for the pain on some nights. Her baby cried so much. Even though she spent her days as a *Madan Sara,* selling vegetables at the market in Petionville's square never netted much money. Situated in front of the cathedral, where the dictator married the Dragon Lady amid a carpet of fragrant white gardenias, the market attracted the rich people living in mansions dotting the hills above Port-au-Prince. After the wedding, the gardenias scattered on the church steps still smelled heavenly for days, masking the rank and rancid odors of rotting garbage and dead animals. The garbage collectors claimed that the big shots, the *gwo nonm,* stole all their salaries. And they wouldn't pick up the trash until the money crackled in their hands.

She rounded the corner into the square. Setting her basket down again, she pulled out the tattered blue cloth that used to be her *mere*'s dress, smoothed it out, saying a prayer to Erzulie for a good day, not too hot, and rewarding with vast sales. The pineapples, she realized, should have been sold the day before, but her breasts leaked every time she heard a baby crying, so she left before she'd sold everything. Maybe a *blan* would buy them.

Despite her prayers to Erzulie, the day dragged by slowly, filled with rich women's maids arguing with her over one *gourde,* bargaining her down. All day. As if one *gourde* would ruin their wallets. She'd learned from her own experience as a maid countless years ago that madams would accuse maids of keeping back money for themselves. Unfortunately, since some maids did just that, their selfishness reflected on all women working in a rich person's house.

Batting away a buzzing black fly, she glanced up from the tomatoes. A scurrying, the sound of feet on the cobblestones, signaled the arrival of an important customer. She spotted the *blan* pulling up in a fancy truck-like car, the color of dust or the skin of a person born to a *blan* and a quadroon.

She'd never seen this *blan* before. An American, this one was clearly not one of those French women who walked through the market with their noses up in the air, sniffing every few meters, dabbing at their foreheads with a lacy Chanel-perfumed white kerchief. Yet, from the angle of the sun, she understood why the *blan* came today. The other street market closed two hours earlier, so the *Madan Saras* there could ride home, up the mountain, on the army truck that traveled to Kenscoff every Thursday.

As the *blan* edged closer to the stack of soft, red tomatoes, she noticed some strange sounds. The *blan* spoke *Kreyòl*, not French! She heard "*Kawots, tanpri.*" With that, ten *Madan Saras* besieged the *blan*, shouting, shoving, begging.

She snatched up the pineapples. Maybe she'd sell them, but the fermenting eyes might doom the sale. A slight breeze blew a piece of brown paper across the pavement, so she seized it and wrapped the decaying pineapples as best she could, hiding the defects.

As she moved closer to her target, she peered over the shoulder of a much smaller *marchand*. The *blan's* wallet opened, thick with a wad of *gourdes* large enough to keep her baby in milk for months. She shoved her way forward, tapping the *blan* on the shoulders.

"*Ananas, Madam?*"

"*Non, non,*" came that voice. "*Mési.* No pineapples."

"*Poukisa?*" she demanded, shoving her bulk against the *blan's* thin body.

Why not?

The *blan* cringed for a moment, then turned and almost ran to the truck. She followed, gripping the pineapples, their juice dripping across her sturdy hands.

When she got to the truck, she stood against the back door and thrust the pineapples under the *blan's* nose. The *blan* opened the back of the truck. At that moment, rage flashed through her, singeing every nerve. There, in the back of the truck, lay enough food to feed a family such as hers for months. And this *blan* wouldn't buy two pineapples for eight *gourdes*?

A baby cried in the crowd that'd gathered behind her. She felt milk escaping from her pendulous breasts. Before the *blan* could close the door and escape back to whatever house existed high up in the mountains, its cool air balmy air perfuming spacious rooms, she grabbed her top, pulled it under her large swollen breasts, and squeezed. Milk droplets showered the food in the back of the truck.

Where there'd been chattering was now dead silence. She stepped back. The *blan* slammed the door shut and raced to the driver's side. Fumbling for the key, shaking. She strode up to that rich woman and thrust the pineapples at her again.

Non, non. Demen mwen pral achte nan men ou.
Tomorrow? I don't believe it.

෨ ෬

The Houngan

The witch doctor never heals his own sores.
~ Haitian proverb

EIGHT WHITE FACES PEERED UP AT HIM. For a second, the reality of his past lives floated from deep reservoirs of memory. Professor, researcher, atheist.

But now, what am I?

A charlatan, as his critics trumpeted, in all the bigwig newspapers? Or a true healer, as the people in the streets claimed?

The cluck-cluck of chickens brought him back to the moment.

Years ago, he realized he could bring a kinder, more authentic understanding of Haiti and Vodou to the innumerable tourists who flocked to Port-au-Prince, those who sought the mystical, the murderous after reading Graham Greene's novel, *The Comedians.*

And that evening, decades later, long after Greene's death, he was poised to do that.

Twelve women in white flowing dresses made of coarse cotton cloth, tightly wrapped head rags hiding their hair, swayed into the circular outdoor room. The whole place, a lean-to really, was held up by thick tree trunks about nine inches in diameter and thatched with palm branches. A cool breeze wafted through the, adding to the sense of the torrid tropics, as did the swishing fans overhead.

And it's all a stage. Yes, it is. Shakespeare was right.

A man strode in, a torn T-shirt hanging limp on his

thin frame, taking his place inside the circle of women. Off to the left, six men straddled large, elongated drums, pounding heart-pumping rhythms. Voices cried out, throats full of sound, mouths opened to receive the rum bubbling in the sequin-studded Barbancourt bottle held by the man in the middle. Sip, spit, blow, the smell of rum soon permeated the air as he sprayed it around with his mouth like a can of window cleaner. Several younger men outside the circle chewed live coals from the fire pit in the center of the room. Then came the glass-eating.

He glimpsed the *blans*, their mouths open to take in the rum, their eyes widening as the man bit into the neck of a flapping chicken and sprinkled the floor with the surging crimson flow. The drumbeats came faster now, and the women passed another bottle of rum as they danced in a frenzy, circling around with locomotive speed, faster, faster.

Through hooded lids, he continued to watch the *blans*, his white hair taking on the sheen of satin in the dim light. Usually, he explained what could potentially happen at a Vodou ceremony, but tonight was different. He kept silent, waiting for their reactions. No explanations, no warning.

Shock, disgust, fear. He saw it all on their faces. And smiled.

The best was yet to come.

A shriek tore through the man's throat as he fell to the ground with the chicken still clutched in his hand. Writhing, movements of a woman in childbirth, screaming, neck muscles engorged, sputtering the name of the *loa* over and over again. Three *blans* jerked and jumped up from their seats, readying to flee the scene. One of the women in white went down, too, quivering in her trance.

Saliva spilled from her mouth, foaming with the frothy whiteness of liquid dish soap. Or toothpaste.

He stared at the woman. This wasn't part of the script, the show meant to be a tourist draw, just that, a performance. A sterile version of the real thing.

The air around him turned chill, despite the day's residual heat pouring off the concrete floor. He stood, walking into the circle, intending to kneel by the stricken woman, verifying her state. Instead, the man with the dead chicken flung the corpse at him, eyes wild, red, and unseeing. Hands clawed at him, and through his now-red eyes, he saw the *blans* leaping from their seats, drinks spilling tiny umbrellas, soaking tablecloths with aged dark rum and pineapple chunks.

More bodies fell around him, powerless to stop the current of madness sweeping through the circle.

Then he fell amidst the twitching bodies and landed face down, chicken blood smearing his cheeks, branding him with color. A voice hurtled through his brain.

You thought you could hide, didn't you? There's no hiding from the Baron in the white palace!

A booted foot jabbed him in the ribs and flipped him over as easily as his mother used to flip cassava bread off the rusty griddle.

Baron Samedi, that's the loa who came that night.

No, not *loa*, real. The tentacles of the man in the top hat, the long black coat, popping eyes behind thick glasses. Those tentacles reached far, even to this place.

Hands thick with calluses grabbed him under his sweaty armpits and yanked him off the ground.

He knew where he was going. Not Fort Dimanche. No.

Hell.

ख़•ख़

THE LANDLADY

Too rich isn't bad; it's returning to poverty that's tough.
~ Haitian proverb

Patting her shining blond hair, the color of polished buttons on a general's uniform, stiff with hair spray, she motioned with her right index finger. The tall, thin maid brought out the dress she'd chosen for her meeting with the *blan*, the American woman renting her uncle's massive house high up on the ridge. She glanced around at her own house, built by her German grandfather for her Haitian-French mother. His portrait hung on the wall in the dining room two floors below, casting his shadow over the family every evening as they dined at the shiny mahogany table. Floor-to-ceiling windowpanes overlooked a garden bursting with white oleander and scarlet hibiscus. Her family tree spread its roots all the way to medieval France, rich with the blood of buccaneers and adventurers who sailed with the soldiers of Napoleon Bonaparte. Then came a short stay in New Orleans after the slave uprising of 1804, but the family returned to Haiti and never left.

She sighed as the maid slipped the floral-patterned, blue silk chemise over her head, thinking of the sugar plantations the family no longer owned. Of course, with her husband's family monopolizing dozens of industries in Haiti, money would never be an issue.

The maid buttoned the back of the dress, starting at her slim waist, all thirty-five tiny, cloth-covered buttons.

It was a dress meant to evade seduction, she chuckled.

What lover would be patient enough to undo every one of them?

Certainly not her husband. She scowled. That morning she'd woken once again to an empty spot in her bed. Fists clenched, she tried to relax into the sensation of the silk caressing her body.

Hurry, hurry. What is taking the girl so long to reach the top button?

A knock on the door brought her back to earth.

The butler bowed, sweat clinging to his forehead. The *blan* awaited her in the library.

I must tell him to use that handkerchief more.

Stepping carefully in her high-heeled shoes, stilettos sharp as a Macoute's knife, she descended the staircase modeled loosely after one in the Chambord chateau. The marble under her feet came from her family's original stately home in the Loire valley. She never tired of telling the story as wine glasses clinked at her massive dining table.

And here she was, talking to a person whose ancestors no doubt sailed in chains from England to the American colonies, as indentured servants, banished for stealing a loaf of moldy bread in London's Highgate. Or whatever.

The butler pushed open the heavy wooden door to the library. The *blan* stood by one of the bookcases, craning her neck to read the titles.

Ah, a book lover. That bodes well for Uncle.

She coughed a small, attention-getting noise. At that, the *blan* turned, a smile lighting up her face, her hand outstretched.

Clammy. Nervous. Oh, dear.

She led her visitor to the sitting room, with the tall, floor-to-ceiling windows overlooking the house's lush vegetation. Watered from the riches stored in five underground cisterns kept full either by torrential summer rains or trucks hauling water from the countryside, the garden meant everything to her. There she'd buried her sons.

Shaking her head to dislodge the ugly memory of that night, she motioned for the *blan* to sit on the brocade fabric of the loveseat. Where the President himself sat when he came with the news of the drownings, the yacht limping back to port, a hole the size of a DFM Captain Camion yawning open on the starboard side. He'd sat with her. The security lights had illuminated his plump, shiny face, not the hot afternoon sun.

The butler stood silently at the door, waiting for her to dismiss the visitor with a predetermined signal. Or to order tea and cake. She turned and faced him, nodding once. Tea and cake it would be.

She listened as the *blan* spoke halting but surprisingly correct French. She learned that the *blan*'s young son was away in America visiting with his grandparents. As for the husband, he'd flown to the Dominican Republic the previous day for some meetings with government officials, about water rights or some such thing.

Tea served and cake passed, she raised the Limoges cup to her lips. That was as far as she got. Crack! The floor shifted as if a giant'd followed the *blan* and shook the house to set her loose. But no.

A tremblement de terre, earthquake!

Eyes wide, the *blan* stared at her, then ran to the door. She followed.

Then the walls collapsed, the broad, dark wooden beams that gave the house its appearance of the past crashed down, pinning them to the marble floor from the French chateau.

She heard screaming, and it was her, her voice.

This can't be happening. It can't be!

She reached for the *blan*'s hand. It was already cold. The *blan* whimpered, eyes shut, breathing rapid and shallow.

She sighed, and felt the cold seep over her, too.

And when the butler and the gardener and the maid sifted through the rubble the next day, that's how they found them.

Hand in hand, for eternity.

ও◌ঙ

ᴛʜᴇ ᴛʜɪᴇꜰ

It's hand in hand they catch the thief.
~ Haitian proverb

The shrieks woke her, before the rooster crowed. Black outside, all she could see as her eyes jerked open.

What is happening?

Tiptoeing to the door, she glanced at her husband, snoring in their bed, one arm flung over the edge. He'd be awake soon, to leave for his job cutting meat for the butcher in the Jacmel market.

Pulling her dress over her head, she slipped her feet into the red plastic thongs she always wore in the house. She picked up the kerosene lantern she kept by the kitchen window. Electricity was widespread in Jacmel, but not on the outskirts, not where she lived, in the poor area.

Again, the shrieks.

She hurried to the door, taking care to raise it by the doorknob, thus avoiding the loud squeak it always made.

Outside, a crowd stood yelling, and she heard the sound of fists on flesh, then clubs. But no one was playing baseball or practicing for a boxing match. She edged closer to the sounds. Peering over the heads of the other onlookers, she pushed her way to the front, for once glad to be as tall and broad-shouldered as a man.

Something warm and wet seeped over her feet, her toes suddenly sticky.

Blood.

"*Sak ap pase?*"

What was happening?

"*Yon vòlè sal!*"

A dirty thief.

She shivered, although the warm night air hung with hot wetness, clinging like a damp sheet spread over rocks in the river where women washed clothes. The punishment for thieves, if caught, meant one thing: death. And not after torture in a prison, police station, or courtroom.

On the streets. At the hands of those robbed. Or those fearful of being robbed.

The man lying on the ground was beyond screaming. Instead, she felt him entering the realm between worlds, where souls lay vulnerable to the spirits. Limbo. Or the danger of becoming zombies.

He moaned. At that moment, the flash of a machete gleamed in the light of her lantern. The weapon's tip sank into the man's chest, grinding against bones. Then the killer seized a rock and pounded the machete's handle with a loud cry and final thrust. The crowd cheered.

On the fringes of the crowd, she spotted a policeman, a known Macoute. He stood there, welcoming a light to his cigarette, from the killer himself. Then, patting the killer on the back, the Macoute sauntered off, down the hill to Jacmel, its lights twinkling, the faint rumbling of the ocean now audible now that the crowd dispersed.

She lurched back to her kitchen and boiled a pot of coffee, hands quivering as she pounded the beans. Her husband stumbled in as she handed him a cup of the hot brew. Sitting in one of the two chairs they owned, he placed new cardboard in his shoes. To cover up the holes, to keep the blood from soaking his feet as he hacked at carcasses all day. Between his job, and her new one, as an assistant to an aid project, they could barely survive.

When she walked into the office later in the morning, her boss pulled her aside. A new *blan*, a woman, would be going with her. To the village, to continue the survey. Best of all, the *blan* owned a vehicle. A big one. No more walking the perilous path along the crest overlooking the white beaches and the ocean views, which people in New York would pay millions for. If only the views weren't in Haiti.

It was a long day. The *blan* could barely speak either *Kreyòl* or French. About an hour before they headed back to the office, the *blan* asked for the toilet. She pointed to the back of the small, dilapidated schoolhouse where they conducted some of the interviews.

Smiling, the *blan* nodded. The purse lay on the table in front of them, gaping open.

Remembering her husband's swollen feet, his sadness after a day of blood and shredded flesh, she grabbed the purse, searching for the money she guessed this rich *blan* had. Over twenty bills, 100 *gourdes* each. Glancing around her, she snatched three, more money than her husband made in a month.

She placed the purse where the *blan* left it.

They drove back to the office in silence.

Her husband wore his new boots to work the next day.

And she never saw the *blan* again.

She wondered if the rich *blan* ever even discovered the theft.

❧

The Businessman

A man's business is a mystery.
~ Haitian proverb

HE WAS A *BLAN*. Then again, he wasn't.

Haiti was his home as a child, the Dauphin sisal plantation his playground, his first language *Kreyòl*, his nannies taking the place of his parents. His real parents lived the partied life of ex-pats of the day, when Barbancourt's dark, aged rum flowed from noon to midnight, ice tinkling in tall etched glasses. Wild, alone, and determined, he became a pilot, thanks to a little war in Southeast Asia. When it came to pass years later, a chance to return to the magical place he remembered, well, he did.

Packing up his Alabama-born fashion model wife and two gangly sons, he flew his Cessna from Miami to Port-au-Prince. There he stunned the customs men, the Macoutes and the *Madan Saras*, with his fluent *Kreyòl*, peppered with colorful words no Haitian dared say in front of their grandmothers.

It was an ordinary early shift on the factory floor he managed, hundreds of women, and a dozen men, sewing slacks for the American market. He watched from the glass cage he called his office. Overlooking the factory floor, he sensed unease among the workers, the union reps whispering in one ear and then another. Something rotten fermented beneath the polite demeanor of all those smiling faces greeting him every morning.

But what was it exactly?

He turned away from the window as the U.S. Embassy's chief spook strode into the room, his hand outstretched in greeting. Behind the pompous fellow, the secretary, his all-around fierce gatekeeper, shrugged her shoulders and slammed the door.

He shook the man's hand, feeling the dampness of the palm, resisting the urge to wipe his hand on his slacks. The two men sank into the plush velvet chairs, purple with gold trim, the sort of thing his wife would never put in their house.

What is he here for?

Instead of speaking, the man handed him a piece of paper, a cable from the State Department in Washington, D.C. His index finger went to his lips.

Silence. Why?

The man from the Embassy pointed to the black telephone on the desk in front of him.

Bugged? How? No one comes into this office except me and the gal out front.

He examined the cable more closely. Something about an Air France plane, due for take-off at midnight. A passenger manifest, too. From the night before.

His head snapped up as he mouthed the names. The spook studied him with a vacant thousand-yard stare, the eyes of a man who'd seen a lot, most of it unmentionable, best kept locked up in a maximum-security archival depository.

He scribbled on the back of the cable, playing the game.

What do you want from me?

The spook took his pen and wrote a few words with a flourish, telling him to finger a couple of people in the factory before.

No, I won't do that. Even if they are Duvalierists.

He stood and extended his hand to the spook. With his hand on the man's shoulder, he walked him to the door. His secretary rushed in, eyes wild.

What's wrong?

He motioned to the spook to follow his secretary to the back door.

A situation needed to be quashed, not with violence, but with words.

The dictator is gone!

Standing on the landing, at the top of the twenty-some stairs, he felt as the Queen of England must have felt waving to the crowds below the Buckingham Palace balcony. He silently thanked all the gods in the pantheon, and his parents too, for his skill with the sharp retort, the subtle manipulation of words, the power of suggestion, the doling out of ill fortune to his listener. In this case, his listeners.

He announced the news in his fluent *Kreyòl*.

The dictator is gone.

Inside, only tears and embraces as the workers realized what the news meant to them, to their country.

Outside, baying like hounds for blood, lusting for a scapegoat, whipped to a frenzy by the rumors and drumming of the night before, a mob blocked the way to the official U.S. Embassy vehicle. Clubs with the heft of baseball bats, rusty machetes, and broken bottles popped up as the crowd drew closer, to hear what he would say, this *blan* who wasn't a *blan*.

Zanmi, tanpri ale lakay ou. Diktatè a pati yè swa, konsa jodi a ou lib. Friends, go home, the dictator left last night.

The crowd went silent at hearing perfect *Kreyòl* from the mouth of a *blan*.

In twos and threes, the crowd dispersed, the one casualty a woman who stepped on a shattered Prestige bottle, the amber-colored glass still reeking of beer.

He took the stairs, two at a time, calling for his secretary to bring warm water and bandages. Taking the woman's foot in his hands, he washed her calloused foot and dressed the wound while the spook tip-toed behind him, then dashed to the waiting car. The driver sped out the gate as the spook waved. He nodded and contemplated the woman.

Men ou pa vreman lib, pa vre?

No, Haiti is not free.

Patting the woman on her shoulder, he trudged up the stairs, back to his glass cage.

And Haiti never has been free. And never really will be.

৵৽

THE DIPLOMAT

When you look at your watch, you will see it's thirteen o'clock.
~ Haitian proverb

Firecrackers boomed on the other side of the chaotic, verdant garden. All the children ran wild, recalling a scene from *Lord of the Flies*, he thought, as he left the residence. Their parents chattered nearby, oblivious to the din, drinking towering glasses of dark Barbancourt rum, well-iced, topped with pastel paper umbrellas mass produced in China. With every pop-pop, he cringed, remembering, his blood pressure soaring as high as those Fourth-of-July bottle rockets. He steadied himself against the white doorframe of the veranda, the terracotta tiles of the patio steaming after the brief-but-torrential afternoon rain.

W. Somerset Maugham's short story, "Rain," came to mind.

How did they ever dry their clothes?

He sucked in his breath, deep and somewhat futile, thanks to the relentless humidity and the clap of firecrackers.

Now is not the time. Not one of those paralyzing anxiety attacks. No!

None of the Embassy staffers at the U.S. Mission to Haiti's annual Fourth of July party spent two days huddled on the floor of the Commissary, cowering behind combat-garbed Marine guards when the dictator left. He'd stayed. Vowing to serve out his appointed term. He owed it to the president. To himself. And to the people of Haiti.

Flinching at another uncomfortably close loud bang, he turned to the man approaching him.

Oh, great. The last person I want to see. Always the bearer of bad, terrible news.

Haiti's minister of internal affairs. The official "responsible for internal security and domestic policy," he recited to himself from the massive handbook he'd memorized before stepping a single foot in Haiti.

Wiping a broad forehead with a black-and-white golf-print Dolce & Gabbana handkerchief, a minister motioned for him to edge closer.

That handkerchief cost more than a Haitian garment worker made in five weeks.

The words startled him, and he stepped back as if snake-bitten.

They found the bodies, Sir. In Hinche.

He thanked the minister, begging off any further conversation by catching the eye of the USAID director, waving at him, to tell him the news.

Since the dictator left, street gangs and drug dealers filled the power vacuum once occupied by the Tontons Macoutes. Actually, he suspected, no, now he *knew*, that Macoutes simply had donned different uniforms, carrying on business as usual. These days, they targeted Americans, angry at the U.S.'s role in exiling the boss man.

Hinche. Situated in the middle of the desolation left behind in Haiti the moment French planters sailed off to New Orleans in 1804. Thereby leaving the survivors to hack out a living while still paying crushing reparations to France, hoping to avoid a repeat of bloodied rivers and flesh-fertilized fields.

It must be the goat people. The bodies. USAID contractors. Oh, no.

Somehow the time crawled by, the firecrackers, the heat, the endless flow of rum quaffed with sweating, icy glasses transported on silver trays glinting in the sun, blinding him. Facial muscles quivering from all the false smiling and back-patting and whatnot. At last, when the final notes of "My Country 'Tis of Thee" faded and the Marine Corps Band put away their brass horns and trumpets, he turned to his wife. She took his arm, his light white linen suit now soaked through with sweat. Together they walked up the four broad cement steps to the house, turned, and waved to the departing, sloshed guests. Most would be eligible for a DUI back in D.C., all squinting into the sun like cowboys in a cheap western film.

Inside the house, they went to his office. First, he kissed her hand as he always did. He then raised his right index finger to his lips and pointed to the veranda on the eastern side of the spacious, no, pretentious house. There, he felt sure they could talk without fear of someone watching or hearing them. Shadows hid them, too, as he recounted the terrible words the interior minister whispered in his ear.

Soon, none of us will be safe. Kidnappings, ransom demands, death if "No" was the answer.

He pushed his wife's chestnut brown hair back behind her ear. She'd be the first to leave, with their children. As he bent to kiss her tears away, his aide knocked on the tall double doors, as ornate as any in a French chateau.

Another cable.

All non-essential personnel must leave. Yes, so it must be.

He handed it to his wife. She nodded, wiping away tears.

Three days later, the massacres began. People in line at the polls, attacked with machetes, slaughtered like animals. Kidnappings.

The beginning of the end.

The two-way radio blared: All non-essential Embassy personnel, to the airport.

I'm essential. Or am I?

ॐॐ

THE MISSIONARY

Life is an automobile without a steering wheel.
~ Haitian proverb

Blan, blan, geev me a dolla!

She couldn't sweep the sounds of their plaintive voices out of her head.

Suppose she'd known before what she learned after only two days in Haiti. In that case, she might still be teaching in a classroom in Akron, watching her first-grade students coloring between the lines, tongues curving along their lips in intense concentration.

But everything changed the night of the church social.

The tall, tan missionary priest with the James Earle Jones voice opened his talk with a short film about health care in Haiti. About his hospital, which he started with the help of wealthy American donors after finishing his residency in both emergency and family medicine.

In the end, not a single person in the audience of over 250 could stop weeping. So much Kleenex, so many handkerchiefs.

Including me.

She slipped one of the brochures about his missionary hospital into her purse.

That very same night, she wrote a letter to the School of Nursing at the local university, requesting an application form. In the mail two weeks later, she found the application forms. So, she checked the endless boxes, filled in the innumerable lines, signed a check for twenty-five dollars, and sent everything to the address on the envelope. Finally, three months later, a fat, precious manila envelope sat in her mailbox. They'd accepted her for nurses training, starting in a month, with a full scholarship and, in addition, a living stipend.

Blessed, yes, I am!

She handed in her notice to the principal of the parish school where she worked as a teacher, one of the few who were not nuns.

After the end of her two years as a nursing student, all the while learning rudimentary *Kreyòl* from a local Haitian woman, she applied to be a nursing sister at the priest's hospital near Port-au-Prince.

And her life changed again with one phone call.

I will be there as soon as I can. Next week? Yes, I think so.

Panting up the potholed, red-dirt, rocky road to the hospital, the Jeep stalled a number of times as it lurched over cannonball-size rocks and knee-deep rushing streams. All along the way, near-naked children darted out from behind the scraggly trees or small hills, chanting.

Blan, blan, geev me a dolla!

When she swore she couldn't endure another spine-tingling bump or the sight of children with their swollen bellies and red-tinged hair, the hospital emerged from a grove of lacy bamboo and swaying palms. Whitewashed, roofed with rounded terracotta tiles, it loomed over Lilliputian vegetable gardens and flowering red and purple bougainvillea.

Crowds of people sprinted toward the Jeep.

The charge nurse, a strapping blond woman who

spoke with a distinct Danish accent, took her suitcase, and led her by the hand down a corridor, a cloister really, over-looking yet more vegetable gardens. No flowers, unless the colorful and edible nasturtiums counted.

Her room recalled photographs she'd seen of monks' cells at Chartreuse in southeastern France. A small bed, no more than a cot, sported a gauzy white mosquito net swinging gently overheard, a graphic crucifix on the wall gazing down on the pristine sheets, a rattan dresser, a three-shelf bookcase, and a large, screened window.

After a supper of red beans and rice in the common room, the priest and the Danish nurse motioned to her. They all headed out the door for evening rounds in the maternity ward, where she would begin working as a mid-wife the next day.

Over twenty women lay in beds, no private rooms, clean, crisp white sheets concealing their bodies, some still swollen with pregnancies, others with squalling or sleepy infants at their breasts. She watched as the priest and the nurse spoke softly in *Kreyòl* with each one, introducing her as they went.

Dimming the lights, run on a gas-fueled generator, they walked across a small clearing to a smaller version of the hospital.

All seemed completely normal and natural. Until they opened the locked door. Down for the night, six women lay in beds resembling those in the main hospital. But the similarities ended there.

She couldn't help but cover her mouth with her hand to hide the shock.

It's like a horror film. But this is no arty film, nor a Wes Craven blockbuster.

Without noses, without fingers, without toes, without ears, six faces turned as the priest murmured a greeting. No babies in sight, although she remembered that leprosy spread through pregnancy or even sexual contact, as AIDS did.

It was too late for these women to regain flesh devoured by the disease. A multidrug regimen cured them, and they would experience no more loss of flesh. The problem was that lepers were still considered unclean, as in biblical days. So, they lived in this place, under the doctor-priest's care, given the dignity of their humanity.

Blan, blan, geev me a dolla!

It was never enough. Never, she thought, as the days and months and years flowed by in one continuous river of memory.

Never.

☜☞

THE ARTIST

If it wasn't for cutting iron, the tinker wouldn't live.
~ Haitian proverb

FEARFUL THAT A CLUCKING HEN or a paper-eating goat would puncture his precious stretched canvases with a peck or a chew or foul his work with urine, he'd ridden all night on the top of a bus, all the way from Cap Haïtien.

At least urine acts as a preservative.

Stifling a lungless laugh, a smoldering cigarette scorching his fingers, he rounded the corner of Roy Street. And stood gape-mouthed on the stairway of the glorious old two-story house with sky-blue shutters, the famed Centre d'Arte, its two shaded verandas overlooking the street, surrounded by crimson-flowering flame trees. Shuffling through a cascade of fallen blossoms, he started up the steps, where all the leading artists of his generation had walked.

And here I *am!*

He tested the door handle with one hand, balancing the art-filled duffel bag in the other, surprised when the door swung open as easily as a flimsy curtain.

His eyes adjusted to the cool darkness inside, dim lighting streaming from the small ironwork lamps attached to the walls. He set the duffel down and stared. He'd heard of the riches found in that old house, once belonging to a wealthy *blan*. But he never imagined such a sight, the startling rainbow effect of so many canvases, so much dazzling color. Even in the spectral white light of night.

Gliding from room to room, guided by the lamps, sighing over the butterflies with filigreed wings side by side with black emerald-eyed leopards and leafy, lacy green bamboo, he explored the house. In the last room, next to the kitchen, he noticed a cot, a torn mosquito net swaying ghost-like in the breeze of a ceiling fan. A note next to the bed invited weary souls to sleep there. From the indentation on the pillow, he surmised that someone had done that.

Why don't I do the same?

He spread the mosquito net, opening it wide enough to slip through with ease, positioning his thin body on the mattress, smelling the hair pomade of a previous sleeper on the lumpy pillow. As he closed his eyes, dreaming of his home in the rugged, treeless, dry mountains of the north, a voice boomed through the room, echoing off the walls, shaking his heart.

Was it real? Or is this place haunted?

The ironwork lamps flickered once, then died, blacked out.

Again, the voice, wishing him a peaceful night.

Only the night guard! Thanks be to the gods.

Hours later, bright sunshine streamed through the cracks in the shutters, and he woke with a start.

Am I dreaming? No, I smell coffee and burnt sugar and papaya.

He stumbled toward the aromas, pulled along by his nose like cartoon characters he'd once seen on a television for sale in a shop near where he lived. In the kitchen, two *blans* close to his age sat at a wooden table with steaming cups of thick coffee in front of them. After drinking a cup of the elixir and eating a bowl of scrambled eggs and fried, ripe plantains, he followed the men into the room with the cot and opened his duffel bag, showing his work to them.

Their faces revealed nothing as they studied the paintings. Nonetheless, he could read them.

Shaking their heads, and not meeting his eyes, the *blans* put the paintings back in the duffel bag. They shook his hand, then turned and walked away.

Non. Maybe next year.

Words he'd heard innumerable times.

Time to leave.

He headed to the port. On a corner near a small, abandoned gas station, he laid a clean yellow towel on the ground and arranged his paintings against the white-washed wall, as he'd seen done in the Centre d'Art. A loud horn sounded as a cruise ship let down its gangplank.

He waited.

Soon a dozen women, *blans*, tourists, dressed in leg-revealing shorts and skin-tight tank tops, walked toward him, exclaiming over the colors, the scenes, the animals in his paintings, signed "Vielot." Like locusts of old, the women snatched up everything, leaving him with enough money to return to his home in the north and back to Port-au-Prince ten times over.

This is good enough for me. These blans don't know any better.

And so it happened that he made a small fortune over the years, his defeat at the Centre d'Art a blessing, not a curse.

And so, too, when the earthquake hit, and the Centre d'Art crumbled like a cracker crunched in a fist, he gave thanks that *his* gallery existed on the open street, the sky overhead a vast ceiling, one that would never crush him to death.

Bondye bon. God is good.

ᕙᕗ

THE JOURNALIST

A gathering storm doesn't necessarily mean rain.
~ Haitian Proverb

The phone rang, late at night, when it's best to be home, in bed. And not alone. The news, the answer to a million prayers.

He'd hurried to the print shop

After hours of frantically writing, and more phone calls to verify facts, he wiped newsprint smudge off his fingers, but missed the spot on his nose, and the one on his chin. Satisfied with the headline and the lead, he gave a thumbs up to the printer. The groans of the rusty hinges of the vintage printing machine faded as he climbed the stairs to the blessed coolness of his office, two steps at a time.

We got him!

He clapped his hands and did a pirouette his ballet-loving daughter would love.

He's gone.

Sinking into his chair, he studied the piles of papers and photographs of his dead countrymen's faces, their bodies tossed into ravines, left as feasts for feral dogs roaming the hills. Many of those faces were journalists who, as did he, wrote words that sank like barbs into the flesh of the powerful.

And the truth got them killed.

He opened the cabinet behind his desk, where he kept his safe and a half-full bottle of Barbancourt's most expensive dark rum, aged fifteen years. He pulled the bottle out, twisted off the gold cap, and poured two inches of the golden liquid into a smudged glass.

To you, mes frères, my brothers.

He drank the whole glass in one go.

Haiti's weather never really cooled down, but that morning the blue sky and gentle breeze off the mountains above Petionville enlivened him. He called his wife and suggested they share lunch at the Cascade, around the corner from the elegant Kinam Hotel. To celebrate the end of terrifying days and sleepless nights.

A knock on the door startled him out of his reverie. A copy of the newspaper appeared, still warm from the press, placed in his hands by a smiling reporter.

He picked it up, the headline on the front page blaring the news of the dictator's departure in large block letters covering the entire front page. Written in both French and *Kreyòl*, the whole issue detailed the sins of the regime, summarizing the living hell people had suffered for thirty long years.

Patting the paper as though it were a sleeping baby, he turned on the radio to hear the news.

And froze in place.

The dictator's voice slunk through the speakers, shouting that he wasn't gone, and had no intention of leaving, standing instead as "firm as a monkey's tail."

My God, what's happening? And what does that even mean, "standing as firm as a monkey's tail?"

He grabbed the phone and called his contact at the U.S. Embassy, confirming the story, yes, it was true. The dictator still slept in the palace. The handset shook in his hand as he set it in the cradle.

My wife! My children! My friends!

Picking up the phone again, his palms damp, he begged his wife to leave, to hide wherever she could. That the next several days would be dire, filled with bloodshed and beatings, death and pain for those celebrating.

He dashed from the office, yelling to the people on the press floor, telling them to listen to the radio, to leave, to hide. Pandemonium, chaos. His heart beating in his chest so hard and so fast he wondered if he would die of a coronary before the Macoutes or the Army found him.

That would be a blessing, yes.

He thought of the envelope that arrived last week, sitting on his desk when he opened his office door, bulging with a steel-tipped 9-mm bullet, a drawing of a coffin. A premonition? A warning?

Of course. Now, today, they will kill me like a dog in the street.

They, the *san manman*, men without true mothers, without conscience, their hearts shriveled as small as the shrunken heads he'd seen at the Musée de l'Homme in Paris.

They would find him. Eventually. The airport shut down, no flights in or out.

He walked down the stairs, for the last time, he was sure of that. No one lurked yet in the foyer of the old French building, its columns a termite's delight, the pink paint peeling off like a *blan's* sunburned skin. It was early, but the morning sun was already bleaching the sky a blinding white. His car started on the first try, praise be. Backing up, he spotted them, the *san manman*. So early, someone must be a mole, but who could it have been? The papers were not yet on the street, the drivers had just left when he heard the awful news on the radio. He feared for them, hoping they would dump the papers and run.

Turning down the Rue de Delmas, he passed the Kinam, its gingerbread-laced veranda sparkling white and chameleon green in the sunlight. Across the plaza rose the Cathedral, and he wished for a moment that he could run inside and claim sanctuary, as a medieval pilgrim would. But the Church held hands, and more, with his pursuers. At the intersection, he stopped to let two *Madan Saras* pass, their babies sucking at the breast as they ambled from one side to the other.

And that pause, that twist of fate, changed everything.

When the Uzis jutted from the windows of the vehicle behind him, he crossed himself.

Holy Mary, Mother of God, pray for us sinners, now, and at the hour of our death.

Pop-pop, pop-pop.

৵৵

The Farmer

Beautiful teeth don't say friend.
~ Haitian proverb

THE *BLAN* SMILED.

And so did she, automatically, as one does when someone else yawns. Her strong white teeth showed for a change, the camera making her sweat even more than usual, despite the unrelenting humid heat of the rainy season. The *blan* with the camera grinned back, thumbs up, and so she relaxed, just a bit.

She motioned with her right arm, welcoming them to her farm.

Small compared to some, one hectare. But she owned something almost more precious than land.

Rising from a spring, water kept her cassava, beans, and corn crops fat and happy.

Praise God for that.

Her farm had something else that others did not. Trees. Mostly mango.

The *blans* behind the man with the camera talked in a language she didn't understand. One of them—a woman as tall as a man—spoke to her in *Kreyòl*, in a funny way, too.

She motioned for them to sit on the benches, out of the sun, under the straw-covered canopy. Then, one by one, they spoke as the woman spoke quietly in her ear, transforming their words into something she could understand.

Credit, what was that? Would a bank own her land if she couldn't repay the loan?

With their help, she would be able to double or triple her production. With irrigation.

She wished he were there to help her, her husband, who'd spoken too loudly one day about the president.

Diktaté. Dictator!

He'd be able to read these *blans*. Their grand white cars and fancy city clothes, not a speck of dirt or grease on them. Their eager grinning faces and uncalloused hands. Just as he'd known the lure of a uniform, the promise of a gun, visions of loot twisted his neighboring small farmers, transforming them into Tontons Macoutes. Loyal to the *diktaté*, the *gros* landowners, and the bishops of *legliz kato-lik*, as cruel as a pack of wild dogs. When those rabid animals heard his voice, thick with clairin one night, despite the truth he mumbled, they dragged him away, leaving him for their kin, the dogs. Right out in the open.

The worst day of my life.

Two of her sons stayed on the farm, while the other three fled after his death. To America, sending the money she picked up at the lotto in Saint Marie every month.

I don't need these blans' money, their credit, their sweetly worded traps.

She shook her head.

In her heart, she could hear him, reminding her of the pigs. When the government barged in, on the advice of the *blans*, and slaughtered all the black pigs. A veritable *dechoukaj*, an uprooting, one that ruined many farmers. And led in part to the large *dechoukaj* after the fall of the *diktaté*. When people loyal to the regime faced their victims, in the streets, in their homes, in their beds.

She thought, too, of *Tèt Ansanm* and the large land-owners who plotted the Jean Rabel massacre. Speak out. Seek freedom. Be killed. Or stay silent. And stay enslaved.

Her land, she owned it, her sweat and tears and even blood watering the corn, the beans. By decree, long ago. By God, she would keep it. Unto the death.

So, no, mési, thank you.

She stood.

Time to go, yes.

She watched them trudging down the hillside, ter-raced for generations, held in place by rough stone ledges. Down to the road, powdery and rutted and narrow, a road that countless politicians promised to pave, but instead pocketed the money for their yachts or their mistresses.

She shrugged.

Kay koule twonpe solèy, men li pa twonpe lapli. A leaky roof tricks the sun, but it does not deceive the rain.

The donkey brayed in its tiny corral.

Overhead, the sun began to hide behind the moun-tain range across the valley. She filled a yellow plastic bucket full of her precious water, hefting it with her mus-cular right arm. Patting the donkey on his soft, breathy snout, she dropped the bucket on the ground at his feet. Then, pulling out a clay pipe, she reached for the shredded tobacco in her pocket.

Taking a deep puff on the pipe, she sighed.

It wouldn't be long before the landowner's henchmen sped up the dirt road and shoved some papers in her face. What the *blans* didn't know was that the landowners con-trolled the bank. *But I do.*

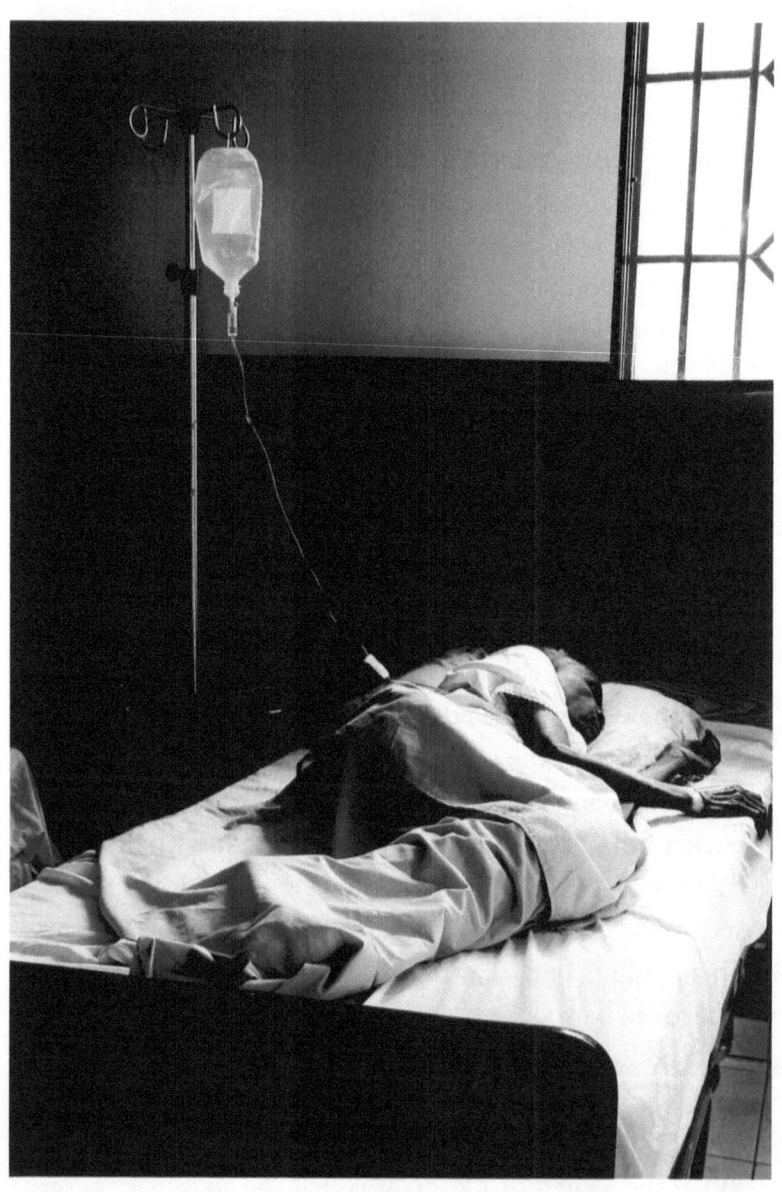

The Doctor

When you are drowning, you grab any branch you find.
~ Haitian proverb

THE THIRD CHILD DIED IN THE NIGHT. He knew there would be more. Many more.

He closed his eyes, swaying on his feet. He longed for the peace of his house, built of wood in the early 1900s by his grandfather, a German immigrant. High up in the mountains, the house still stood, although a few windows broke and the veranda crumpled. The quake swallowed everything else around it. He couldn't leave the hospital. Or what remained of it. Debris, bodies, and vehicles blocked roads, and bridges collapsed.

When disaster struck, when the land shifted, when the crashing of stone and soil beneath the relics of man took down not just buildings but also dreams, futures, hopes, it was as if a giant fist punched through the earth's crust. Or a furious army marched through, burning and bombing everything in its wake.

The sun rose the next day, as always. Yet for one moment, gazing upward at the pink sky of the sunrise, the lazy milky clouds puffing by, the birds chirping, perched on the branches of shattered trees, it seemed as if nothing had changed.

But it had. Everything had.

He wiped tears from his sagging eyelids. The sound of voices behind him, urgent, called to him. Ten nurses stood along the wall, none daring to go inside what remained of the hospital. Dozens of patients lay on bare ground in the open air. Flies embedded themselves in oozing blood, sniveling starving dogs darted in to lick at festering wounds, beaten away by those strong enough to resist. The dusty air above them rang with the moans and whimpers of those still trapped in the wreckage.

The eeriest thing about the morning, though, was the great silence. Aside from the birds and the moans of the wounded, nothing made a sound. Except for the buildings still dissolving into the wounded earth, the aftershocks terrifying the survivors, cringing in fear with each rumble, huddling in the ruined streets where they took refuge.

Exhaustion overtook him, and he sank to the ground. Resting against his car, now tilted into a sewer ditch on the side of what had been a busy road, deserted except for the people streaming past, bloody T-shirts and ragged shorts concealing their thin bodies, their blood, or someone else's.

With his eyes closed, he appeared as dead as all the others lying in the street or pulled from the rubble. Something poked him, tentatively, and he sensed hands rummaging in his pockets. Thieves, or just desperate people trying to find something to barter, something to sell, something to eat?

What? Maybe I am *dead.*

The thieves yelped in fear and fled as he stood, wobbling on his tired legs.

He noticed the nurses hovering over a woman lying on the ground, a sheet under her, blood seeping between her legs. Another woman giving birth, in what should be a joyous time, now one of sorrow. The petite nurse, as big as his sixteen-year-old daughter, motioned him to come, quickly. He gripped his well-stocked medical bag, which he carried with him everywhere, and hurried over to the woman.

One glimpse at her transformed him into a fortune teller: the mother would not survive, nor would the baby. A crushed pelvis jump-started her contractions, but the size of her abdomen told him the baby was not due for four more months. A hopeless situation. He listened to the baby's heartbeat, weak but barely discernable. Then, shooing the nurses away, he rummaged in his bag for syringes and two vials of morphine. Leaning over the terrified woman, in shock and not feeling the full brunt of the pain that would overtake her in seconds, he filled the syringes quickly. Taking care, he injected her under the armpit, where the dark, dense hair would mask the needle marks.

She opened her eyes for a second as the morphine began its lethal trip to her heart, reaching out to touch his face. Smiling, she mouthed, "*Mési*." Thank you. Her eyes closed again. He felt for her pulse in her neck.

Nothing. Good.

What he'd done would remain between him and the gods he believed in.

Four children dead, among thousands and thousands of other souls.

In the schools, in the houses, in the streets, crushed in concrete and debris. Built of crude cement, bought from the lowest bidders, the rest of the money pocketed by the rich and powerful. Each contract signed foretold a death sentence.

Yes.

Because of their greed, he'd violated the oath he'd sworn the day he first donned the white coat.

But surely mercy counted as "first do no harm" sometimes? Pitye, pitye.

৵৵

The Prisoner

Don't uncover a kettle that isn't boiling for you.
~ Haitian proverb

A TINY SPARK OF JOY FLICKERED in his despair-filled heart when he found himself on the road to the notorious Fort Dimanche prison. Four of his friends crouched on the rough benches inside the black truck, one of the dreaded police vehicles that scooped people up, usually for no good reason. In broad daylight sometimes. Though usually at night, with violent pounding on the door, terrorizing those sleeping inside hovels or mansions. It made no difference.

If you speak out.

No crusading journalist, he. Nor a disgruntled businessman. And definitely not a renegade priest, offending both dictators and bishops.

Just a man with an opinion.

The first night was the hardest.

Crammed into a space wide enough to touch the walls with outstretched arms and long enough to lie curled up on the cold, wet, slippery cement floor. A floor mottled with old blood, vomit, urine, and feces. A bed of lice-infested rags in one corner and a rusted Folger's coffee can in the other. For the necessaries of life.

Why am I here?

He waited, day after day. Nothing. Then it became year after year. Never a trial. As for lawyers, none dared demand justice. Or they would languish in cells side by side with their clients.

The heat kept him awake at night, as did the mosquitoes. Then the malarial fevers came and went. The guards laughed when he begged for quinine, or even an aspirin. Rattling their nightsticks against the bars, they walked down the corridor, whistling, cigarettes burning long ashes close to their thick fingers.

And the worst of it, despite the sickness, the death, the neglect, happened when the *blans* from various Human Rights Commissions paraded past the cells. Taking notes, no photos allowed, talking with the most recent prisoners, those with flesh still padding their bones, no scars marring their smooth-shaven faces, their fingers straight, and their fingernails clean, not bloody, not missing.

And one day, there was Tiko, yelling in broken English and French, about the mistreatment, endless deaths, and unrelenting torture, when the guards paraded the latest *blans* from France outside the cells. The next day, Tiko's naked, bullet-ridden body sprawled in the middle of the parade ground, genitals cut away, throat slashed, eyes gouged out. He looked away as he marched by with the rest of the prisoners.

The message, oh so clear: talk earns death, not freedom. Silence *was* golden.

I am a coward, taking the blows, the swinging belts, keeping silent.

But he lost count of the deaths as one day melted into another. And another.

Then something changed.

He remembered the exact moment. Watching a

cockroach crawling across his bare chest, he thought of the films he'd seen in school, his ribs protruding as badly as those of concentration camp victims.

The iron door rattled. Puzzled, he wondered what it was. Too early for the rotten beans and rice and overripe plantains he ate once a day.

A new guard stood at the door, the warden behind him.

They gestured for him to follow them, grabbing his arms as he stumbled in his weakness.

Is this it, then? All that waiting and suffering, for death anyway?

When they stopped walking, he swayed in the prison yard, in front of the gate where the black truck dropped him off all those years ago. An ambulance idled on the other side as the gates swung open. A *blan*, a doctor, stood there, his stethoscope clacking against his chest as he and two orderlies ran toward him, pushing a gurney. They gently helped him onto the clean, crisp white sheet and loaded him into the ambulance. The gates to the prison clanged shut as the ambulance's siren started up, squealing, red light flashing.

He never learned why he spent years mired in the bowels of the most feared prison in the country. But he did know one thing. Tiko saved his life. Like a game of dominoes, Tiko's witnessing led to other voices and still others, until the words ricocheted, reaching the ears of those who could open doors with just whispers.

And now, I scream for people like Tiko.

৵৹

THE TORTURER

When you are in the slaughterhouse,
you must accept blood splattering on you.
~ Haitian proverb

THE WOOLEN HABIT ITCHED. Sighing, he shifted in his first-class seat, buckling the seat belt tight across his fat stomach. Gazing across the aisle, he noticed a tiny boy with ice-blond hair and deep blue eyes. He smiled at the child. The boy didn't smile back but stared at him, wide-eyed, tiny mouth quivering.

He knew that look well.

Fear.

He turned away, pulling on the starched white wimple pinching his plump cheeks so tight he could barely catch his breath.

In an hour and a half, I will be in Miami!

He watched the economy-class passengers as they struggled through the aisle, loaded down with enormous suitcases, pet dogs, and crying babies. Feeling his upper lip, smooth as a mango from the painful waxing of the night before, he didn't see the man who stopped and squinted at him, then went on by, wearing a puzzled expression.

He sighed again. Remembering.

The day the news spread with the speed of a gasoline fire. The dictator gone, flown out on a U.S. Air Force jet to France. Leaving them all to their fates, at the mercy of infuriated mobs chanting in the streets, crying for blood and revenge after thirty years of hell.

And I am one of those they hunt.

He never meant to be who he became, who he was. Still, the thrill of closeness to power, money, women, and palatial homes in Port-au-Prince and Miami won out over the decency his washerwoman mother taught him. As a devout Catholic, his current garb would sadden her no end, would strike her as blasphemous.

He tugged at the cord digging into his ample waist.

And thought of another cord, about the same thickness, with the same heft. Strong enough to strangle a man much taller than he. That was his first kill, in the bowels of Casernes Dessalines. Then, in one of the small cells, not much bigger than the stall in a public bathroom in the Miami airport, the floor of black cement perfect for hiding the inevitable blood stains, he crossed from innocence to murder and eternal damnation.

Murder. There's no other word for it. I know.

But then, another story unfolded in his memory. One laced with communists, insurgents, and scum intent on ruining the lives he and others of his ilk built, at unfathomable cost to their souls.

He'd wrapped the cord around the man's neck, a man whose name he never learned, just the prison number. Naked except for the same underwear the condemned man wore when dragged into the prison, stinking with the odor of a rapacious dog that'd rolled in something dead. Grime coated that face, grease-like, eyes empty, not even fear. Twisting the cord with a thick baton, yes, he'd done that. A higher-up officer taught him, using a technique taught at the School of the Americas at Fort Benning,

Georgia. He marveled at the quickness of it, the precise-ness. Of course, it helped to have the prisoner shackled and cuffed to a table.

No flailing arms and jutting legs to slow the inevitable.

A shout and ensuing commotion snapped him out of his thoughts of his days torturing prisoners in the name of the dictator.

He glanced up.

A man pointed at him, thick neck veins swollen and bulging, yelling his name so all the people on the plane could hear it.

Behind him, the pilot frowned, golden wing pin and epaulets shining in the sunlight streaming through the windows, refusing to fly if he didn't go quietly.

Then the Army officers arrived. Young, not yet cor-rupted. Their Uzis pointing at his head, they gestured for him to release his seat belt and stand. The man shouting grabbed the wimple, revealing his close-cropped hair and telltale sideburns. One of the soldiers cuffed him.

So, this is how it went for them all.

The small boy across the aisle buried his face in his mother's lap.

Tripping over the nun's habit, he stumbled down the aisle to the plane's door, avoiding the other passengers' shocked, covert gawks. He stepped into the afternoon sunshine to the sound of clapping and cheering.

A black truck awaited him at the foot of the stairs.

The driver shoved him into the back. The foul odor of vomit filled his nose.

And fear, too.

I was just following orders! I was, I was!

THE BEGGAR

Better to work than to beg.
~ Haitian proverb

HIS HANDS WRAPPED WITH FILTHY RAGS, he scooted close to the line of *blans* waiting for a tap-tap. Seeing them recoil at the sight of his small wooden board, roller-skating wheels attached in the four corners amused him. Or perhaps it was the glimpse of his tiny, withered legs.

Life changed for him when a *blan* missionary spotted him dragging his thick, muscular torso up and down the road in front of the brothel. Using his arms and hands to propel himself forward, hands outstretched to all and sundry, begging for a few reluctantly proffered coins or dirty paper *gourde* notes. With the wheels, he could move around, plying his trade in parts of the city near and far.

The gawks, the guffaws, the finger-pointing. He no longer cared. Money was money.

Long ago, he'd accepted his fate.

The gods punished his mother, a whore murdered by a powerful drug dealer. When his mother died, the French brothel owner offered him a roof over his head and food to eat, speaking to him only in French. One of the other whores taught him to read French. Thus, in the evenings, he read and traveled far from the dusty, garbage-strewn streets of Port-au-Prince to far-flung places of wonder and sophistication.

But he still went out daily and paraded his wounds, his deformity to the world.

But the *blans* in line intuited none of this.

Motioning to the well-dressed women waiting in line, he rolled up to the tall, blond *blan* Catherine Deneuve look-alike. A blustery wind blew her shining hair across her heart-shaped face as he tapped her foot with his long delicate fingers. She gawked at him, but no words left her gaping mouth. He held out his other hand, then motioned to his mouth, miming a deaf-mute, making his saddest face, tears in his eyes, thanks to the bar of Ivory soap in his pocket. She carried one of those woven, colorful bags from Kenya, which made his life far easier. Plunging her red-tipped fingers inside, she pulled out a roll of grimy *gourde* notes from a burgundy-hued wallet and handed him a 100 *gourde* note. Then she put the wallet back in the bag.

Cheap! Maybe she doesn't know the exchange rate?

But he'd accomplished his task. The well-dressed ladies at the back of the line pushed their way forward until they stood directly behind her. One jostled her and asked a question in broken English. As the *blan* answered, the other woman thrust a hand into the Kenya bag and fished out the wallet. No one saw, no one noticed a thing.

Least of all, the *blan*.

He waved as he sped away, a grin lighting up his face.

Hours later, his partners in crime walked in with over US $200 in *gourdes*. Laughing, they spread the money on the table in the brothel's office.

The owner patted him on the head. And motioned to a man standing in the shadows. A Macoute, to whom they all paid a cut of their daily takes. Opening the wallet, the Macoute barked in his guttural voice, hoarse from clairin and Cuban cigars, yelling at prisoners and other lowlifes.

Discard the wallet? Why? How? Where?

The wallet belonged to a U.S. Embassy secretary. Not people his father wanted to anger.

The next day, one of the beggars, or thieves better said, hitched a ride on the very same tap-tap, commanding the driver to return the wallet to a guard at the Embassy.

Of course, the money wasn't there, but still.

As usual, he left the brothel the following day, propelling himself along the road, his hands wrapped in the same filthy rags to heighten the effect of grinding, unrelenting poverty, seeking his next marks, reeling them in with pity and horror. Shoving the bills and coins they showered him with between his useless legs, he hummed "Haiti Cherie" with the rhythm of his arms as he crossed streets and dodged the legs of passersby.

A la bon peyi se ti Ayiti! Such a good little country, Haiti!

Fate brought him to that life. It could be so much worse.

Yet the *blans* would never believe that.

Wi! Yes!

౸ఠ

The Fisherman

The fish is not friendly with the net.
~ Haitian proverb

HE YANKED AT THE ROPE, the sparkling clear water below the color of a *blan's* blue eyes. And chuckled. In the trap, he discovered six large lobsters wrestling each other. It would be a good night, some bottles of clairin and wild dancing and maybe something more. For the tourist boat was due soon at a sandy white beach, not far from where he'd anchored. Six lobsters meant he might find more in a trap closer to the beach.

Thanks be to God.

Grabbing his worn, but precious oar, carved from the wood of a mango tree, he paddled his narrow wooden boat with deep, sure strokes, startling the schools of yellow and blue fish nuzzling the pink coral below. Finally, he reached the spot where he'd left another trap. Frowning, he noticed slippery pools of oil covering the surface of the water here and there, remnants from the myriad tourist boats on their way to Mikaz Beach. Once again, he set the great sail arching over the boat, the whiteness that of a large pelican's wings.

Anchoring the boat, he scraped off flecks of rust from the make-shift anchor. He'd fashioned it from a piece of an abandoned car he'd discovered on a trip to the mainland, the year his father disappeared into the hell of Fort Dimanche, the year the dictator's father seized power.

Depi lontan. A long time ago.

Engine noise brought him back to the moment. He gripped the rope of the trap, hoping the frayed spot would hold until he had time to repair it. With some sisal, which hung from the rafters of his cinderblock house, a blessing. Most of his fellow islanders lived in flimsy huts created with this and that, debris washed up from the sea.

Four lobsters!! Ten, to sell to the blans.

The tourist boat rounded the end of the island, skirting the small flat rocks jutting from the surface, skimming over the water, swooping with the grace of a great white seagull. He spotted about fifteen *blans* hanging over the brass railings of the ship. One sick, and there usually was at least one. Even on calm days.

Their clean, white shorts and colorful T-shirts contrasted with his own grey, sweat-stained wife-beater. Waving to the ship's captain, he trimmed the sail and paddled close to the bow. One of the Dominican seamen held up his hands, asking how many lobsters. He held up ten fingers.

Dis. Ten.

The deckhand pulled the traps up and emptied them into a large metal drum barrel. He heard the lobsters rattling around, futilely straining to escape. The trap returned with his money in a plastic bag. He grinned and waved.

A small blond boy on deck waved back.

He watched the child as the parents, also blond, hoisted him down to the clear blue water and walked to the beach. His lobsters also ended up on the beach, as did numerous other types of fish, gleaned no doubt from his fellow fishermen. They lived perilously on large flat rocks cropping up from the sea, in huts constructed of slats and bamboo fronds, paddling their dugouts under their own power, not by the wind.

The aroma of roasting beef filled the air as the *blans* frolicked in the warm, translucent water. His stomach clenched with hunger, which he sated with a few pieces of boiled cassava dipped in the sea for the salt.

That smell, so good.

The *blans* devoured more food in one hour than most islanders ate in a week. When they finished, or thought they had, the Dominican crew member who'd paid him gestured for them to walk back into the water.

Balancing crude wooden trays holding cut-up limes, the crew served broiled lobsters, cooked on iron slats on the beach over a hot charcoal fire. Breaking off the heads and dipping them in the salt water, the *blans* chewed, as he had done with his cassava, squirting the pieces with lime before popping the bits into their mouths.

Then they clambered back onto the massive boat. Laughing and chattering, ignoring the women sitting in the meager shade of the prickly shrubs lining the bleak, treeless hillside behind the beach, paying no attention to the intricate necklaces made of pink coral and tropical seeds the women hoped to sell.

He shook his head and set the sail, following the boat to their next stop, a small village where people lived on the generosity of tourists.

A handful gourdes for those baubles, not much, not for them!

The tiny blond *blan* sat on his father's shoulders as they climbed down from the boat. Then it started, the clamoring, the beseeching, the grabbing. Recoiling, seven or eight of the *blans* splashed through the water, hurrying to the boat. Hands reached out to touch the boy, ruffling his hair, while his father held on tight to a pair of tennis shoes, worth several months' wages on the island.

They didn't see the old man, toothless, limping, barefoot, eyes on the shoes, grabbing them, knocking the father down. The boy, too. Off the old man ran, into the maze of huts lining the beach.

The boat captain grabbed a rifle and jumped from the boat, headed to the huts.

But the *blans* screamed.

No, no!

The captain cursed in Spanish

Maldito.

The big boat turned around and left, the wake splashing against the sides of his tiny white boat.

He adjusted his traps. Placing the precious money in the pocket of his shorts, he headed home, wondering if the old man ever wore the shoes. Or did someone steal them from him?

Lavi a difisil. Life is hard.

಄ఞ

The Hotelier

Memory is a sieve.
~ Haitian proverb

JACMEL, SHE SOON LEARNED, behaved as no other city she'd ever known. For one thing, there was Carnival. For another, the art. And yet another, the crystalline-blue sea. Which lapped at the edge of her French husband's property, a hotel built in the curvy crescent of a white-sand beach.

Why do tourists thrill to the words "white sand beach"?

And now, years after she first stepped foot in the town, a naïve young English girl with a first from Oxford in English literature, Carnival loomed again. As high as the mountains encircling the once-isolated city. Filled with clapboard houses garnished with iron filigree, Jacmel seemed for all the world to be a street in New Orleans's French Quarter.

She stood on the balcony of room 25, inhaling the tang of ocean air, pleased with the patio below. Two dozen tables, pristine polished cypress imported from the marshes of Florida, each festooned with bright red hibiscus flowers.

They'd all be dead in the morning.

Grimacing at the sight of ratty, brown palm fronds littering the gray gravel walkway, she clenched her fist so hard her long crimson fingernails drew a few drops of blood. All must be perfect for the elderly Germans arriving on that cruise ship from Miami. Then, scurrying through the hotel's three wings in the rushing manner of the White Rabbit in Lewis Carroll's *Alice in Wonderland*, she peeked into each room, noting either perfection or flaws.

Gardeners! Maids! What did it take to do a job right?!

Germans were the worst guests, but she expected that, given the culture's propensity to record even the most horrific atrocities in wartime. A speck of dirt, a misplaced fork, a burnt-out lightbulb, she'd never hear the end of it.

But Carnival allowed her, and the staff, leeway.

Masks and costumes, often thrown together with odd bits of clothing filched from aid barrels, lent a sense of anonymity lacking in daily life in Jacmel. Riotous and vulgar, and often terrifying, with elements of Vodou lurking below the surface, threats of violence seeping out here and there, masked figures disappearing like crabs into their holes at the beach. Carnival tested her nerves every year.

She made a mental note to ask her husband to hire two more guards from the ranks of the known Macoutes, so loyal to him, he who left no palm ungreased.

Yes, those monsters still exist, falling into the power vacuum left by the dictator. Fear still gets results. Most of the time.

In the kitchen, she collared the maids, admonishing them about the imperfections in their work. She took a moment to speak with the gardener about the palm fronds. After the tongue lashings, she sat at the staff table, gesturing to the cook. A cup of tea appeared near her hand. She drank, thinking of England, the coolness, the yellow and white roses her father grew. Wiping her forehead with the napkin under the teacup, fortified by the familiar taste, she headed to her husband's office with a most unpleasant task, asking for more security for the guests due in two hours.

Fear. It grows here like mold on a wall after a flooding rain.

Wiping her sweaty hands on her skirt, she knocked on his gleaming reddish-brown mahogany door. His harsh voice boomed behind it, bidding the intruder to come in. Softening his tone when he saw it was her, she told him what she needed, citing the rumors circling in the kitchen about the protests in Port-au-Prince.

Now the menu. Not too much spice or pepper, but a taste of the Caribbean, yes.

All too soon, the guttural sounds of German drifted through the halls of the hotel. Hysterical laughter crescendoed as the beer flowed, followed by dancing and other antics. As she announced dinner, the crowd quieted and followed her to the patio. Featherlight breadfruit fritters arrived first, followed by red beans and rice, pork griots seasoned with *epis*, French baguettes, and *pikliz*, all dishes similar to German tastes. Strudel, at the end, concocted with mangoes, not apples.

More drinking, then cries to take to the street, to mask up.

She watched as they left, grateful for a split second of quiet. Leaving the clean-up to the staff, she climbed the stairs to her suite of rooms, at the far end of the third wing of the hotel. A quick prayer escaped her lips as she settled into bed.

Please let all be well.

When the pounding on the door began at 3 a.m., she glanced at her husband, who'd slipped into bed at midnight, unbeknownst to her.

What is going on?

The police burst into the room, aiming their Uzis at her husband, screeching at him to stand up and turn around, quietly. Handcuffs clinked as the men arrested him. With no explanation at all.

She phoned people she knew all day, seeking news of her husband, begging them to tell her why he'd been arrested.

That night, the last the Germans would sleep at the hotel, she sat in the kitchen, tears welling up as the cook plied her with tea and the small lemon cakes she loved. As she sipped her tea, the cook slouched across from her, patting her hand. One of the German women limped in at that moment. Aiming a finger at her, the woman muttered that Madam's husband worked for the *Milice* during the war, rounding up Jews and torturing people, pointing to her own damaged leg as proof.

No, no, he joined the Resistance. Didn't he?

The woman shook her head. And hobbled out.

The Restaurateur

It's the kitchen that tells me how the house is.
~ Haitian proverb

Dut, dut, dut, the bullets smashed into the street side of the whitewashed wall. Just a few crazies practicing. He ducked anyway since his head skimmed slightly above the spot where wall and sky met. He checked his watch. Opening time in twenty minutes. Truth be told, he didn't expect any customers. The thought no sooner left his brain than they walked in, a group of four, three men and one woman. *Blans*, foreigners.

Early, new to the country, probably with one of those medical NGOs.

Definitely not accustomed to eating fashionably late.

He smiled and beckoned for them to sit at the table closest to the frilly palms, the shade more pronounced there than on the other side of the courtyard. To drink? Water, of course. Sparkling. Wine later. He handed out the ornate, but simple, menus of the Lebanese dishes he took so much pride in. Even the Dragon Lady had eaten at his table once, so close to the cathedral where she'd married the dictator, that fat, childish, spoiled man.

Surveying the courtyard, he made his way to the kitchen for bottles of fizzy water. He remembered his restaurant in Beirut, before the troubles began, where people could speak and write with freedom not known before. Now he recognized the same trends in this place of such remarkable beauty and unending tragedy.

Best not to dwell on what I can't change.

With a deft movement, he popped off the tops of the water bottles, the sound faint but so like the now-silent guns, the gunmen moving on to other, more vulnerable targets.

Maybe tonight there will be silence. Maybe.

He sighed, notepad and pencil ready for taking orders of baba ghanoush, hummus, lamb brochettes, and salad. The cook would be pleased with the simplicity of the dishes. Crusty old man, he. Too old to be a chef now, but how could he, the son, dictate to the father?

Stubborn beyond imagining!

With the arrival of the food, the guests fell upon it with tiny cries of pleasure. They ordered two bottles of red wine. And brandy, too.

In the kitchen, he stopped and sat at the table in the middle of the hustle and bustle. Prepping for the next day's customers, if there even were any. Taking inventory or scheduling a wedding or even funeral meal for long-time customers. Or, worse of all, checking the receipts. He imagined, as his father did, that they'd have to close if business didn't pick up. All the civil unrest scared customers away.

He stood to check on the *blans*, as predicted, the only customers of the night. When he asked if everything was alright, they smiled the smiles of people who needed some peace after a week or so of tending to starving children or treating the aftermath of gunshot wounds or setting the broken bones of a beating.

The telephone rang. His father didn't hear it, his deafness now so profound that hearing aids did little. He sprinted into the kitchen and grabbed the receiver hanging on the wall. A cousin yelled excitedly on the other end.

Curfew! At 8 p.m.!

The clock on the kitchen wall showed 7:50.

Dashing into the courtyard, breathing hard, he waved his hands, yelling for them to leave. Ten minutes remained before they needed to be off the streets or be shot on sight. He gazed at their pale faces, now the color of that whitewashed wall, eyes wide as a deer's in the headlights on a lonely country road. Scrambling for their wallets, they threw fistfuls of money on the table and ran with the gait of frightened rabbits to their 4WD trucks.

Sirens wailed in the streets below. The harsh blasts of Uzis ripped through the balmy evening air. He bowed his head and prayed, something he'd not done since leaving Lebanon.

Lest some beggars spy the cash on the table through one of the bullet holes in the wall, he darted over, bending low, and grabbed the money they'd left him. More than enough to cover everything they'd eaten and drunk.

I hope they are safe.

He returned to the kitchen, telling his father what had happened through pantomime and a loud voice. The old man regarded him, saying, of course, they would return, for the restaurant's gracious hospitality always drew people back. This curfew wouldn't last forever.

But he had his doubts.

I hope you are right, Baba.

৵৽৽৶

The Humanitarian

*Watch your bones so that you don't step on
"if only I had known."*
~ Haitian proverb

She regretted wearing stiletto heels the minute she stepped from the Embassy limousine, the ambassador's flags firmly attached to the headlights. The liveried driver jumped out to open the door for her. Around her sprawled acres and acres of what she'd call a shantytown, for the lack of a better word. The poorest slum in the poorest country in the world, she'd been told. Cité Simone, named after the dictator's elderly mother.

And as the ambassador's wife, she was expected to show an interest in the country's people. Not just the wealthy oligarchs, but the poor as well.

No plants, no trees, nothing green to remind people that this was a tropical island, the potential always there for lush, thick, leafy foliage. Like her garden high up in the hills behind Port-au-Prince.

Minutes away from the port, the ocean, waves lapping languidly against the pillars where cargo ships docked. Airplanes took off for the wider world mere yards from the edge of the encampment.

Row after row of hovels spread out before her. She nearly rapped on the limo window to stop the driver from leaving her there. The fetid stink of oozing mud and open sewers in the gutters assaulted her nose, her perfume a poor warrior losing the battle against the stench of rotten food, animal bodies, and feces. Thick charcoal smoke added to the odiferous mix.

A voice called to her. She turned. One of the Spanish nuns, of the order of St. Vincent de Paul, reached out to her. Shod in practical black shoes with laces firmly tied, the nun beckoned to her, a warm smile on her sweaty face.

She shook the proffered hand.

How do they stand it?

She followed the nun into the church, which she hadn't noticed, so dumbstruck had she been by the sight of Cité Simone

She'd long since lost her faith in a supreme being.

How could a loving, benevolent deity allow this to happen?

Despite the ministrations of the sisters, their hospitals, their schools, their day-to-day efforts to better the people's lives, nothing seemed to have changed in their ten years of toil.

That cemented her conviction that there was no God, at least not the benevolent white man with the blue eyes hanging on crucifixes everywhere, or so it seemed.

Souviens que tu es poussière. Remember that you are dust.

Scenes flashed through her mind of Dante's Inferno or one of Hieronymus Bosch's more gruesome paintings as she hurried through the narrow passages of the slum. Grateful for the Vick's nasal inhaler the nun had pressed on her, she plodded on through the human rat maze. Shacks stretched as far as she could see, constructed from bits and pieces of tin, cardboard, rags sewn together, whatever the owner could find, much as magpies make their nests.

Rounding the corner onto a much broader swathe of

the slum, she saw the hospital and her limousine ahead. She dabbed at her face with a tissue, fighting the urge to run, and longed for the cool, clean rooms awaiting her at the enormous house on the hill, a universe away.

The sound was faint at first, but then she heard it more clearly the closer she got to the end of this nightmare.

Blan, blan.

She stumbled for a moment. The nun caught her by the elbow.

Darned high heels.

She looked down as something tugged on the hem of her dress. A toothless woman sat with both legs in the gutter, inches away from the filth flowing toward the sea. A baby lay in the woman's thin, scarred arms, eyes as dull and lifeless as those of day-old fish on ice in the local markets. Unwrapping the filthy blanket covering the pitiful little body of a baby girl, the mother pleaded in *Kreyòl*. Puzzled, she turned to the nun for translation.

The nun hesitated, then told her that the mother wanted her, the *blan*, to take the child, to give her a better life than she could.

I can't do that. What can I do? What can anyone do?

In the limousine, she couldn't get the image of that child out of her mind. The tiny face haunted her sleep for several nights. Finally, she phoned the nun and asked about the child.

Dead? Oh no.

The nun assured her that the child was dead when the mother pleaded for help, adding that it was impossible to save everyone, for it wasn't God's plan.

But, unfortunately, even if there is a God, His message gets lost in the roar of sobbing.

᨞᨞

THE ANTHROPOLOGIST

The yam vine follows the pole.
~ Haitian proverb

He grew up an outsider, in a culture believing only blue-blooded Bostonians or silver-voiced Virginians counted. Drawn to the underdogs, people on the margins, he found no reason not to step out of the box, flipping the bird as it were to the rank-and-file anthropologists, those on the inside.

On the ship's deck, he filled his pipe with prime Virginia tobacco and puffed, the smoke briefly obscuring his view of the mountains rising above the sparkling blue sea below.

The steamer approached the port, a pounding wake surging behind it, upending a small fleet of small fishing boats, knocking them over as effortlessly as pins in a bowling alley. He frowned. Watching the fishermen frantically trying to save the morning's catch solidified his belief that *blans* didn't see what they needed to see.

They never really see it, although it's right there, in front of their eyes.

It was poverty, systemic oppression, ignorance. He could go on forever with examples. But he wasn't preparing a lecture, no. He was there just to observe, take notes, record, synthesize, and sympathize.

Down the gangplank, once again on land, his legs mimicked the gait of a cartoon sailor. As he made his way through throngs of beggars yelling *blan, blan*, hands waved in front of his eyes and fumbled with his tweed jacket. The odor of sweat, smoke, and stale beer hung heavy in the air as he tripped over a rough board, his albatross of a suitcase slowing his way.

So much like Africa! Yes.

He spotted the tall, smiling man at the edge of the worn wooden dock, leaning against a bullet-hole-studded wall. The man's height was noticeable among the crowds of people at the port, most stunted by malnutrition or the immense, heavy loads tied to their backs, charcoal, wood, donated clothing, and even a black pig or two. His colleague for the following year. Another anthropologist, native to the country, his translator and drinking companion. Their shared love of Barbancourt rum had brought them together at a faculty party in New York City.

His friend pointed to a rusty green taxi idling at the end of the dock. The skinny driver ran around to the trunk, popped it, and tossed in the battered leather suitcase, handling it as if it weighed no more than a four-pack of toilet paper. He recalled how heavy it was, filled with the thick, precious volumes necessary for his work.

He gazed out the dirty window as the taxi sputtered through the wide, grimy street, the Grand Rue, speckled with vendors selling every possible item a shopper could desire. And even some they didn't yet know of. The heat and the grit soon overtook all his senses, so much so he dozed despite the potholes every two yards, his spine taking jolts that would stun a soccer player. He woke to the sight of a large sign, resembling those he'd seen stretching over entrances to ranches in the American West, immortalized in films. But, instead of "Rancho Bonito" or some such thing, this one read "Verrettes."

The taxi skidded to a halt in front of a church of limestone and pink concrete. A crowd gathered around, peering through the taxi's smudged windows

It's a gauntlet, only I am not a captive. Or am I?

A priest, short, white, his fleshy countenance flushed a light purple from the midday heat, rushed out from the darkness of the nave, welcoming the newcomers in strongly accented French. Gesturing for them to follow him, he led them down a path to a small building off to the side of the church. Red brick and wood, sturdy, the house was a welcome change from the minuscule ship's cabin where he'd spent the last two days. At 10 that night, after a meal of cornmeal mush and fat, shiny red beans, and some chunks of fried plantain, his friend clapped him on the back and left for his own house, three streets away.

Morning dawned early, as it always did in the tropics, one second pitch black, the next blinding with sunlight and crowing roosters announcing the start of a new day, like it or not.

Thus, the rhythms of his year began in earnest. Traveling rutted roads, swallowing road dust, beating back mosquitoes, shaking in his blankets with malarial fevers, recording music and words and faces and Vodou ceremonies few *blans* had ever seen, much less attended as special guests.

There, he soon learned, lay beliefs about the cosmos. Ideas came to fill his thoughts, day and night, experiences he puzzled over again and again. He distanced himself from the Vodou men, as skeptics called them. It wouldn't do to appear too drawn into the ceremonies, frothing at the mouth, shaking with the *loa* riding one's haunches. "Going native," his fellow foreigners termed it dismissively, sniffing with sounds of disdain.

But one night, his defenses down, malaria crawling through his veins, he succumbed to the call of Papa Legba. He stepped over the door sill into the realm of black magic, *maji nwa*. And the rite of Petro, too, the same force that fueled the Haitian slave revolt of 1804.

A year to the day he'd set foot on Haitian soil, his friend, the tall man, went searching for him, scouring the hillsides around Verrettes. No one knew where he'd gone. Rumors flew far and wide of a white-haired *blan*, who flitted through the forest, seeking a way home.

Here? Or here? There? Or there?

৵৽

THE WRITER

A parrot never forgets its first master.
~ Haitian proverb

The voices cackled, close to his ear. Or so it seemed to him.

Que fais-tu ici? Que fais-tu ici? What are you doing here?

He craned his neck, searching for the people speaking. The only signs of life were two enormous macaws, crimson plumes topping their heads like soldiers wearing fancy-dress French military uniforms. Hidden among the rippling leaves of the flamboyant trees, the birds squawked as one of the gardeners poked the trees with a long pole, the one used to clean the swimming pool. Indignant, perhaps, the birds flew off to another tree in another verdant garden.

No matter what those men do to that pool, it's always murky, dark enough to hide a body or two.

From his perch on the veranda in front of his spacious room, the turret chamber, the bloody one, he could see down the tree-lined street all the way to the port. He turned his attention to the rum punch at his elbow, famous all over the Caribbean, the drink that launched firestorms from the pens of a multitude of writers who'd stayed in the hotel.

Some reported their sleep interrupted by ghosts, wailing, and general mayhem. Though it could well have been the booze talking.

And the specter of a murdered president, too.

Not surprisingly, the hotel was fully booked. For the first time in a decade, gunfire and death always being good for business, quipped the owner, when he signed the guest register and checked in. Uprisings tend to bring out the locusts, the fence sitters, and the morbidly curious. The international press. They sniff out stories like a dog aiming his nose at the sweet spot of another of its kind.

Indeed, what *was* he doing there, in the very same place that'd hosted such literary luminaries as Malcolm Lowry and Graham Greene and Truman Capote?

Parrots sometimes posed the right questions.

The chatter of the press rose from the floor below, laughter and guffaws, boasting in that hotel of writers. Perhaps he could wheedle the owner into letting him stay in the other turret room, far from the madding crowd? At least the breezes, if any, would cool him down faster than where he slept now. Despite the ceiling fans, the rooms could be blisteringly hot some nights.

And no one would admit it, but closed, locked doors at least kept some of the bogeymen out. Or at least the rattling of the doorknobs would alert the sleeper.

Why am I here?

Drifting off for a moment, lulled into sleep by the intense heat and bleached white sunshine, he leaned back in the rattan chair, white as the hotel's exterior. Charles Addams featured the hotel in several of his cartoons. Macabre, those drawings. The hotel oozed with a sensation of something sinister.

No, not because of the various trappings of Vodou on the walls. Although the sculpture of Agwé, Vodou

god of the sea, painted red and blue and stuck in the en-
tryway, caused him to hesitate each time he passed it on
the winding staircase. No, instead, it was a killing, brutal,
inhuman. Years ago. Forgotten by those young journalists
carousing down below.

And he wanted to know if such a murder would be
repeated.

Positively medieval. That was his first thought when
he read the decades-old report in the London *Times*. How,
using the only weapons they had, their bare hands and
the machetes they swung day after day in the sugar cane
fields, the mob came for the man, the president, whose
family built the hotel, their home at the time. Chased him
up to the turret room.

*Blood stains must still be visible under the rug, I wouldn't
doubt.*

Hacked into pieces, essentially drawn-and-quartered,
body parts pierced with metal poles, held aloft through
the city to the cheers of chanting crowds.

What gets lost in the story is yet more murder. The
brutal massacre of over one hundred political prisoners,
shot, mutilated. His sympathy lay with them, not the fall-
en president who'd ordered the bloodbath. So fraught did
the situation become that the Americans sent in the Marines, who stayed for fifteen years.

And here he was, right in the middle of yet another
uprising.

He walked down the stairs to the bar.

Let the Danse Macabre begin!

The young bartender, crooked teeth crowning his

grin, shoved a rum punch at him across the mahogany bar that once served the American Marines as a pool table.

No, not that.

Instead, he gestured to the bottle of Johnny Walker Black sitting high up the shelves, its shoulders sporting a thick coating of dust. No ice, or he'd be asking for dysentery on top of everything else.

Smooth. The rich, thick, well-aged liquid slid down his throat, silky and harsh simultaneously.

He raised his glass to the bartender.

Plus ça change, plus c'est la même chose! The more things change, the more they stay the same!

৵৽

THE EX-PAT

If the dog tells you what he sees in his dreams,
you won't go out at night.
~ Haitian proverb

THE VOICE CRACKLED OVER THE WALKIE-TALKIES.
Thankfully, the U.S. Embassy finally allowed contractors
to access the things. The news sputtered, coming out rather garbled but clear enough.

The provisional government called for elections in
two weeks. Behind-the-scenes chatter among the Haitians' good-old-boys network and the Embassy created a
roster of candidates. The usual suspects.

Sometimes that radio is such a nuisance.

One day, a diplomat signed in with a question about
whether she should drive her car or not over a downed
electrical wire two blocks from her house. The ensuing
merriment raised people's spirits a notch.

But not for long.

She folded the blanket into a small compact square
and put it in the closet in the long, empty hallway, windows facing west, where sunsets blazed. Gazing up at the
misty mountaintops surrounding Kenscoff, a mini-Swit-
zerland of the rich and powerful, or a Simla, more like,
she counted her blessings during the quiet hours of the
warm afternoons.

Below, the guests reclined on chairs, the massive patio
open to the clear, late afternoon sapphire-blue skies. The
maid passed around replicas of the famed planters rum

punch so beloved by ex-pats. Many chose instead to upend endless bottles of Johnny Walker Black while huddling in groups of three or four, gossiping and laughing.

What is going on?

She turned away, meaning to join the crowd below. But something caught her eye. A flash, a glimpse of something dashing across the hillside. One of the Marines sensed it as well, shouting for everyone to get inside, into the great room, to get down, and lie on the red, terracotta tiled floors. Glasses of punch and scotch shattered on the patio as they ran, the wetness seeping into the concrete, sizzling a bit in the residue of the day's sunshine.

Radios burst into life, voices babbling, guns cocking, people crying, dreading and knowing what might be lurking out in the scrub.

After ten minutes, the *chop-chop* of a helicopter droned overhead. The co-pilot leaned out and gave the all-clear signal, a thumbs up.

People stood in small groups, shaking, as she searched wildly for him, her husband.

Where are you? Where are you!?!

Across the room, near the kitchen door, the bookshelves stuffed with cookbooks cast an eerie shadow. The sun was moving closer to the sea, barely visible from the balcony off their bedroom.

He ran to her, and she thought he'd break her back, he gripped her so hard. The rest of the guests raced for their cars, where their drivers cowered beneath the undercarriages, their once-immaculate uniforms now splotched with engine oil and tiny glittering rocks, like confetti tossed about at a teenager's Sweet Sixteen party.

Left with the chaos of that frightening moment, they stood silently amid the broken glasses and plates, bits of food strewn about, facing each, clasping hands still. The three dogs padded carefully through the shards and licked plates. She shooed them away, patting each on the head, cooing promises of bones and more. They scattered to their favorite spots in the garden, the papaya tree that never fruited, due to its being a male plant. The red bougainvillea struggling, waiting for the rains late that year. The tiny flamboyant tree reaching for the top of the wall, but never quite succeeding.

The radio sputtered again.

What now?

The voice droned, unemotional, used to giving orders, expecting them to be followed, not questioned.

A curfew for nonessential Embassy personnel until further notice.

One week passed, lethargy, the hopeless feeling of prisoners locked behind walls. One week left until the elections. Violence far worse than when the dictator left. Barricades of burning tires, gunshots nightly, gasoline shortages, food shortages.

Then the radio clattered on again.

Evacuate.

Get to the airport. Bring important papers. One small suitcase per family. U.S. Air Force troop planes would be standing by at 07:00 hours.

Fear. There it was again.

She always wondered what people grabbed when

faced with disaster, with the need to flee.

Now I know something about what it is to be exiled.

That last night, they heard the rat-a-tat-tatting of gunfire, the whimpering of their dogs, the sobbing of the maid in her tiny airless room below stairs.

When the sun exploded over the horizon the following morning, they dressed, then gulped down the stale remnants of a baguette. She stood at the kitchen door, hugging the maid, both weeping. Then, urging the maid and the gardener to take what they could before the house was ransacked, she wiped away the tears on her cheeks.

Fear. Such a crippling emotion.

She felt the wet nose on her calf before she saw it. The black dog, the one with an uncanny intelligence, the one who whined when she left for the market, driving the 4WD over the rutted road down the mountain. Stooping, she pulled the dog's face toward her, kissed the quivering head, tears wetting the white streak between its ears.

You know, don't you?

He honked the horn. She smiled as best she could. Then dashed to the car.

The gate opened. They started down the mountain road, the potholes and the rocks exposed after every rainstorm slowing their progress, but not much. She turned, like Lot's wife, and she wished she hadn't in the years that followed.

The black dog raced behind the car, barking, howling. She sat back against the seat. And howled, too.

☙ ❧

THE PRIEST

The witch doctor says he pulls people from the mouth
of the grave, but it's God who does the healing.
~ Haitian proverb

THE SOUND OF THE *BOKOR*'S SCREAMS still woke him at night.

Even though the fiery death occurred three weeks before, the horror of it also populated his every waking thought. Yet, his priestly vows, his oath to protect the confidentiality of the confessional, kept him from going to the police. Besides, everyone imagined the police were on the take, in bed with the powers that be.

And that included the Church.

He was different. Unlike most Westerners, and Catholic priests, who dismissed the tenets of Vodou, he didn't. He'd seen genuine signs of its veracity. After all, didn't he put his own faith in an unseeable and untouchable god?

Who am I to judge?

That Sunday, he woke early, as he always did before saying Mass. It was the fourth Sunday in Ordinary Time. He based his homily on the second chapter of Zephaniah:

> *Seek the Lord, all you humble of the earth,*
> *who have observed his law;*
> *seek justice, seek humility;*
> *perhaps you may be sheltered*
> *on the day of the Lord's anger.*

If everyone mumbled about police corruption, they

also gossiped about who killed the *bokor*. Beau Rivière, on the banks of a dry stream bed, mere yards from the turquoise-blue ocean, measured a kilometer in diameter from beginning to end. Hordes of people fled after the *dechoukaj*, when the townspeople and the Church demanded justice, however tiny. Many Macoutes, also *bokors* or *houngans*, joined the exodus, hightailing it to Port-au-Prince. There, no one recognized them or knew of their mendacity, their malevolence.

But I know who killed the bokor.

People filed into the sanctuary, a small thatched-roof hut, its concrete walls strong enough to withstand the countless hurricanes and tidal surges plaguing coastal towns such as Beau Rivière, especially during the sultry summers. Drums, the same ones used in Vodou, welcomed the congregation. Men dressed in their best, dark suits, the ones in which they'd be buried. The women in clean white blouses and crisply starched headscarves all the colors of the rainbow.

In his homily, he dove right into the sin and the evils of revenge, taking his cue from Romans.

For the wages of sin is death ...

As he spoke, his eyes roamed the crowd, seeking the killer. Finally, the aviator glasses gave witness. The man in the back pew.

The soothing rituals of the Mass ended, with him at the doorway of the church, shaking hands with the faithful. And some not so faithful. All their joys and sorrows, he buried them in his heart. Their evil deeds as well.

Then came the last person waiting to shake his hand.

The man in the sunglasses grasped his hand and murmured in his ear. The man's body odor, tempered by the aroma of vetiver-scented aftershave, wafted through the air as the priest struggled to pull away. But the man leaned in even closer, smiling, showing tobacco-stained teeth, and swung an arm toward him. Pulling away the starched white guayabera shirt covering a pistol anchored to a plump, soft fleshy waist. The scented air brought back that hot and humid day, mid-afternoon, when a man slipped into the confessional booth, mouthing those ancient words, "Forgive me, Father, for I have sinned."

I smelled burning rubber, too, with every word that man breathed. So, I know the man's another bokor, a witch doctor, just like the dead man.

Whistling, the man turned and walked with a jaunty step toward the dusty road, tipping his white Panama hat in farewell.

The inviolable secrecy of Confession derives directly from revealed divine law and is rooted in the very nature of the sacrament, to the point of admitting no exception in the ecclesial or, even less so, in the civil sphere.

Those words tied his hands and silenced his tongue. The Church was his life. What else could he do but minister to the least of these, the most vulnerable? And try to overlook the heinous crime.

Yet, the screams woke him night after night, his dreams swimming with taunts and with specters. No amount of praying kept his anguish at bay.

Dear God, you have forsaken me!

He grew thinner as the weeks passed, his appetite diminished, and his hair turned greyer with every passing hour. Or so it seemed. His housekeeper gossiped with the women at the stream as they washed clothes and shared stories that kept life spicy and exciting, even in a small place like Beau Rivière. A handsome *blan* priest supplied hours of entertaining prattle. They realized what ailed him, daring not to speak above a whisper, none of the usual laughter, the incessant banter.

Dare I believe I'm possessed? Cursed?

By hiring another *bokor*, the man with the sunglasses unleashed the dark spirits, *maji nwa*. Black magic. Making sure the priest never revealed that vile act. The priest's housekeeper suspected he had no idea his sickness stemmed from *maji nwa*, none at all. She took it upon herself to counteract the *bokor* by consulting a *mambo* she trusted. Her own mother.

The doll appeared on the man's fence post one morning, its heart pierced with a silver needle, sunshine filling the valley, drying the misty fog. By evening, the killer lay on the linoleum floor in the hallway. The house, bought with the blood of so many, became a coffin. The right hand covered the heart.

No one entered the house, fearing all the *maji nwa* there.

That same day, the priest heard his stomach rumbling, and asked for pork griots, rice, and red beans. Thus, the following Sunday, he stood behind the altar in the small church filled with fragrant yellow flowers

and preached the words of Luke's gospel on the eighth
Sunday in Ordinary Time:

> *A good person out of the store of goodness*
> *in his heart produces good,*
> *but an evil person out of a store of evil produces evil;*
> *for from the fullness of the heart the mouth speaks.*

❧❧

THE RESTAVEK

Money is a devil.
~ Haitian proverb

THAT MORNING WAS DIFFERENT. Somehow, some way, he sensed it. He'd heard his mama and aunt praying the night before, not to the white man hanging on the cross, but to the *lwa*, the other god, Papa Legba.

On their bed, he noticed a white plastic bag, labeled with big black letters, from the *boutik* on the corner. He bummed candy from the old woman there, with promises to sweep the dirt in her front yard once a week. Usually, on Sunday, when she went to Mass and closed the *boutik's* doors for an hour.

His clothes, clean and neatly folded, filled the bag.

He lived with his mother, his aunt, and his six brothers and sisters on one hectare of barren land in a tiny, thatched hut smaller than the pig pen.

A shiny black car stopped in front of the hut, honking its horn, sounding like a cow caught in the brambles that served as fences. A tall *blan* stepped out, dressed in white from head to toe. Tipping a Panama hat to his mother, the man spoke in a torrential flow of *Kreyòl*.

How could a blan speak that way?

But a closer peek at the man's hair told him another story. Not a *blan*, but close.

The man handed his mother an envelope stuffed with *gourde* notes. She looked around, checking if any nosy neighbors were plowing with their mules in the field nearby. Seeing none, she stuffed the fat envelope into her brassiere, patting it with the same gesture she used with his littlest brother, still a baby.

She motioned for him to come out of the house and bring the bag of clothes with him. He stepped into the sunlight, revealing his own lighter skin, the legacy of a French planter several generations back, the man who'd owned the land now divided among the descendants of the slaves who'd burned the big house and skewered the planter, his wife, and their children with rusty bayonets. In 1804. The nuns at the school taught him that.

I love school, learning to read, writing stories.

All that ended when his papa died in a bus accident six months before. The driver tried to pass another bus on the narrow stretch of road, a few miles away from the village. Both buses hurtled to the bottom of the ravine and burst into flames. He closed his eyes every time he went by, sure he heard his father's ghost moaning.

The man in the white suit motioned for him to get into the car. He turned to his mother, with surprise written on his face. She wiped her eyes with her sleeve and hugged him.

I'm going to live with this man and his wife in Port-au-Prince?

And he would go to school and live a better life than she would in this small village.

The promise of more schooling lifted his spirits a bit.

Sliding into the car's back seat, he ran his hand over the cool leather. Another man sat in the driver's seat, staring at him in the mirror. The man in the white suit slid in too.

He waved to his mother. As the car raced away in a stream of dust, he turned for a last glimpse of his home. His mother sank to the ground, arms flailing in the air, his aunt leaning over her, grabbing her, bringing her close.

Like a blackbird in flight, the car sped over the road. The air inside felt how he imagined France to be, at least from the books he'd read at school.

But why did the man give Mama that money?

Seeing the road in the car was different from what he'd experienced while walking. Soon, he didn't recognize anything. The ocean lapped against the beaches off to the right, sights he only knew from books and the stories his father had told him. Soon the countryside melted away. All he saw were houses packed together like little boxes, with people poking their heads out, like the pigeon houses his grandfather built from odds and ends, scraps he found in the street.

The car pulled into a long winding driveway, a house as big as a church up ahead. No, far grander than a church, much grander. More like one of the palaces in his books. The driver opened the door for the man in the white suit. Then motioned for him to get out, and fast.

The man loped up the stairs to the veranda, where a woman stood, also dressed in white, with pale skin like the man's. She kissed the man on his cheek. They walked into the house, wrapping their arms around each other.

The driver shouted at him to move, pointing to a path off to the side of the driveway. As he walked toward it, a woman wearing a dirty apron and headscarf appeared. Grabbing him by the shoulder so hard he almost dropped the plastic bag of clothes, she propelled him to an open door, the kitchen entrance. Pointing to a corner in the sweltering room, she signaled for him to leave his bag with the shredded rags. Then she shoved a broom at him, gesturing to the floor.

He thought of the prayers to Papa Legba, the money in his mother's bosom. So, too, the story the nuns told, of thirty pieces of silver and a man on a cross.

Oh no. Oh no.

Weeping, he swept. He realized what he was. A *restavek*. A slave by another name.

☙❧

THE GANGSTER

*A dog doesn't eat plantains, but he doesn't want
a chicken to peck at them.*
~ Haitian proverb

He raised his left hand, the first two fingers twisted into a Star Trek-like signal, resulting from burns inflicted on him by a gang of Tontons Macoutes when he was ten. Screaming at them for gouging out his father's eyes in front of him, he'd pummeled the Macoutes with his small fists. Enraged, they grabbed him and thrust his hand into the cooking fire, his flesh sizzling like a chicken leg.

*Then one of the Macoutes shot Papa. Mama sobbed for
years.*

And now he was one of them. Almost.

With his other hand, he waved his AR-15. Balancing on the pile of garbage, he slipped on an oily bottle filled with ants. They were busy slurping at the sweetness inside after days in the brutal heat of the tropical sun. The camera bobbed up and down in front of him. He slid sideways. Grimacing, slicing across his throat with his damaged hand, he yelled at the cameraman.

Cut, cut!!

Again, he climbed up to the top of the foul mound, motioning to the five bulldozers lined up along the edge of the garbage pile. With a ripping sound, the engines hummed and sputtered. Shifting gears as one, the drivers moved forward slowly, tentatively, as screams crescendoed behind him, reminding him of a noisy crowd at a soccer match.

Tin roofs and cardboard walls wrinkled like tissue paper as the giant machines crept through the garbage piles and started their work, revealing the truth behind their presence. Demolishing the primitive dwellings, the bulldozers crunched everything in their path.

Gunmen loyal to him marched through the narrow alleyways of the slum, determined to shoot anyone resisting, anyone supporting a rival gang. Bullets sprayed everywhere as women grabbed their children, filling plastic bags with whatever they could cram together at such short notice.

He moved toward the crumbling sea wall, watching.

A film, the scene reminds me of one. Which?

The cigarette in his scarred hand burned close to his fingers, and he flinched, the gunfire fading behind him.

Papa. Mama. Children crying.

Shaking the cigarette, he tossed it into the trash at his feet, where it smoldered, then blinked out as the oozing, rotting garbage extinguished it.

Just like a life. One minute, there. The next, not.

He jumped down from the wall and strode over to the stalled bulldozers. By now, they'd razed over a hectare of land, dotted with small fires where cookstoves still burned, mostly charcoal, but some gas.

Babies cried in some of the ruined shacks. Women's wails echoed in others as his men attacked those vulnerable female bodies. He lit another cigarette and asked the cameraman to see the video.

Perfect.

Giving a thumbs up, he signaled it was time to post

it all on his website.

Whistling, he waved to his chauffeur, parked a block away from the carnage and chaos. The black limousine, small black and red flags attached to the fenders, glided through the streets, up Delmas, through Petionville, into Kenscoff, verdant, forested, cool, air clear and fresh, erasing the stench of garbage and rot in his nostrils. He gazed at the stucco wall surrounding his house, the iron gate filched from an old, ruined chateau in France, the guards dressed in black, their AR-15s gleaming in the afternoon sunlight. As the car rolled onto the grounds, the gate clanged shut. He dozed for a moment as the car drove up the mile-long driveway.

Now for some champagne. And the news.

The shouting roused him.

He gripped the pistol in his belt, one he'd taken off his first kill at age twelve. When he'd left for dead the cocky Army private who'd pulled it on him. The private caught him stealing weapons from the battery near his childhood home in the slums.

He raced into the house, catapulting himself up the steps two at a time, praying no one had infiltrated the compound in his absence. He trusted everyone around him.

But should I?

His wife stood at the top of the curving staircase, sobbing, hair disheveled, her dress soaked with tears, her phone shaking in her hand. Pointing at it, crying. News of the bulldozers, the video, him on the pile of stinking garbage, the dead children, raped women. Not on his website, no, but on the television.

Then he knew. The cameraman. Traitor.

Every man has his price.

AFTERWORD

ON JANUARY 1, 1804, enslaved Africans in Saint Domingue overthrew their French masters. Since then, for almost 120 years, Haitians have celebrated that daring fight of their enslaved ancestors, a prolonged carnage halting the rule of their French masters. Putting an end to slavery on their side of Hispaniola, the island they share with the country now called Santo Domingo.

At this writing, Haitians still wake every morning to the threat of violence. Now, danger comes not only from earthquakes and hurricanes but, once more, from their own people. Gangs, not Macoutes ....

It seems fitting to end this brief, fictional journey into Haitian culture with the "Soup of Freedom," or *Soup Joumou*. During years of enslavement, Haitians watched as their masters relished a soup enriched with beef and vegetables, akin in many ways to a modern-day French *garbure*. This soup became *the* dish to cook and eat on January 1, a symbol of what it cost their ancestors, and them, to gain their freedom.

Soup Joumou should also be known as the Soup of Hope. Haiti's children and young people must have hope in order to dream of the future, despite the uncertainties of the present moment.

Soup Joumou

1 ½ pounds beef chuck, cut into 1 ½-inch pieces

½ cup vegetable oil

1 medium yellow, chopped

1 stalk celery, roughly chopped

4 cloves of garlic, peeled and minced

1 teaspoon dried thyme

1 large scallion, diced

6 – 8 cups chicken stock

Fine sea salt and freshly ground black pepper to taste

2 malangas, peeled, chopped into 2-inch cubes

3 medium carrots, peeled, sliced ½-inch thick

2 turnips, peeled, chopped into 2-inch cubes

2 yams, peeled, chopped into 2-inch cubes

2 butternut squashes, peeled, chopped into 2-inch cubes

Half a medium green cabbage, sliced

2 russet potatoes, peeled, chopped into 1-inch cubes

1 6-ounce package vermicelli

1 tablespoon tomato paste

2 tablespoons *epis*

1 scotch bonnet pepper, left whole

Parsley, chopped

Fry beef in oil until well browned in a heavy gallon-size cast iron pot. Remove meat from pot and set aside. Stir in onion and celery; cook until onion is translucent. Add garlic, cooking for 30 more seconds. Toss in thyme, scallion, and chicken stock. Return meat to the pot and bring to a boil. Lower heat, cover, and simmer until meat is getting tender. Season with sea salt and freshly ground black pepper. Remove meat from the pot once more. Add the next seven ingredients and cook until tender. Using a blender or food processor, puree the vegetables. Stir in the vermicelli, the tomato paste, the *epis*, and the scotch bonnet pepper. Simmer until pasta is al dente. Add more stock if the soup is too thick. Do not puncture the pepper while stirring. When ready to serve, remove the pepper, add the meat, and heat through. Check seasoning. Serve garnished with parsley.

Bay kou bliye, pote mak sonje. The culprit forgets, the victim remembers.

*Citizens, not less generous than myself,
let your most precious moments be employed
in causing the past to be forgotten; let all my fellow-citizens
swear never to recall the past; let them receive their misled
brethren with open arms, and let them, in the future,
be on their guard against the traps of bad men.*

~ **Toussaint Louverture**, hero of Haitian independence

GLOSSARY

Agwé. Vodou god of the sea.

Baron Samedi. Vodou god of death.

blan. A foreigner, regardless of origin or skin color.

bokor. Witch doctor. Practices with "both hands," meaning for both good and for evil.

boutik: A small grocery store selling basic household items.

Casernes Dessalines. Army barracks in Port-au-Prince and site of interrogations. Named after Haitian general Jean-Jacques Dessalines, who led the Haitian revolution against Napoleon's army and served as emperor from 1804 to 1806.

clairin. White rum, a cultural icon in Haiti.

Comme Il Faut. Haitian cigarette brand.

Damballah: Vodou serpent god, revered as a loving father figure.

dechoukaj. To uproot, or tear down, refers to events after Jean-Claude Duvalier fled Haiti in 1986.

Delmas, Rue de: Major thoroughfare in Port-au-Prince.

DFM Captain Camion. A small truck weighing about 1,500 pounds.

Diktaté. Haitian Kreyòl for "dictator."

djon-djon. Tiny black mushrooms, usually served as a rice dish, *Djon-Djon* Rice.

Duvalier: The last name of François Duvalier (Papa Doc), dictator of Haiti from 1957 to 1971, followed by his son, Jean-Claude Duvalier (Baby Doc), who ruled Haiti from 1971 to 1986. Their followers are called Duvalierists.

epis: A seasoning made from celery, parsley, onion, garlic, and peppers. Similar to the Holy Trinity of New Orleans cuisine.

Fort Dimanche. Notorious fort used as a prison and interrogation center under the Duvaliers.

foxglove. A highly poisonous plant, *Digitalis purpurea*.

Eruzlie Freda: Vodou goddess of love and beauty.

gourde. Haitian monetary unit. One US dollar to 117 Haitian *gourdes*. (Fall 2022)

houngan. Male Vodou priest.

Iron Market. Central market in Port-au-Prince, with distinct, lacy design of iron meant for a rail station in Cairo, Egypt. When authorities there cancelled the order, the edifice was shipped to Haiti after Haitian president Florvil Hyppolite bought it in 1891.

Jean Rabel massacre. Killing by large landowners of over one hundred peasants demanding land reform on July 23, 1987.

Kenscoff. Town in the mountains north of Petionville, site of much truck farming and homes of wealthy Haitian families. Similar to Simla, a town in the Himalayas where the British went to escape the heat in colonial India.

Kouzin Zaka. A being similar to the boogeyman of childhood dreams.

Kreyòl. French-based Creole language spoken in Haiti.

Laboule. A suburb of Petionville, high up in the mountains.

loa. Lwa in Haitian *Kreyòl*. Spirits, gods.

Madan Sara. Vegetable vendor.

maji nwa. Black magic.

mambo. Female Vodou priest.

marchand. Vendor.

Milice. French paramilitary organization active in World War II, in cahoots with the Nazi-leaning Vichy government.

necklacing. The practice of placing an old automobile tire around a person's neck, filling the tire with gasoline, and setting it alight.

NGOs. Non-governmental organizations, generally nonprofits.

Papa Legba. An intermediary between the gods and humans. Vodou god.

Petionville. Wealthy suburb of Port-au-Prince.

Petro. One of two groups of Haitian gods. Considered to be hot, aggressive, and associated with black magic.

restavek/restavec. A child whose parents, or others, receive money in exchange for the child to work/live in wealthier households. A modern form of slavery.

School of the Americas. A military training center at Fort Benning, Georgia, where U.S. military personnel trained officers from Latin America and the Caribbean in counterinsurgency techniques, including torture. Now closed.

sisal. Plant grown in the north of Haiti and on La Gonâve island. Used to make rope and twine, but used in other ways, such as paper, fibers, and mattresses. In the past, large plantations covered thousands of acres.

spook. Slang for spy.

Tèt Ansanm. Political party in Haiti.

Tontons Macoutes. Volontaires de la Sécurité Nationale (VSN, Volunteers of the National Security), a paramilitary group started by Papa Doc in 1959 that terrorized the Haitian population for decades. The name comes from that of the Haitian mythological bogeyman, Tonton Macoute ("Uncle Gunnysack").

USAID. The United States Agency for International Development, a branch of the State Department.

Vodou. Religion derived from African spiritual practices by enslaved people.

BIBLIOGRAPHY

Balch, Emily Greene, ed. *Occupied Haiti.* New York: Negro Universities Press, [1927] 1969.

Berendt, Tom. "Celtic Origins of *Bosou Twa Konò*: Creolization and Appropriation of the Three-horned Bull in Haitian Vodou." *Journal of Haitian Studies* 26 (2): 31-52, 2020.

Cadet, Jean-Robert. *Restavec: From Haitian Slave Child to Middle-Class American.* Austin: University of Texas Press, 1998.

Comhaire-Sylvain, Suzanne. "Creole Tales from Haiti." *The Journal of American Folklore* 51 (201): 219-346, 1938.

Cope, R. "'We Are Your Neighbors': Edwidge Danticat's New Narrative for Haiti." *Journal of Haitian Studies* 23 (1): 98–118, 2017.

Danticat, Edwidge. *After the Dance: A Walk Through Jacmel, Haiti.* New York: Vintage, 2002.

_____. *The Butterfly's Way: Voices from the Haitian Dyaspora in the United States.* New York: Soho Press, 2001.

Depestre, René. *Hadriana in My Dreams: A Novel.* New York: Akashic Books, 2017.

Deren, Maya. *Divine Horsemen: The Living Gods of Haiti.* London: Thames & Hudson, 1953.

Diederich, Bernard. *Seeds of Fiction: Graham Greene's Adventures in Haiti and Central America, 1954-1983.* London: Peter Owen Publishers, 2012.

Dubois, Laurent. *Haiti: The Aftershocks of History.* London: Picador, 2013.

Duck, Leigh Anne. "Rebirth of a Nation: Hurston in Haiti." *Journal of American Folklore* 117 (464): 127-46, 2004.

Fievre, M.J., ed. *So Spoke the Earth: The Haiti I Knew, the Haiti I Know, the Haiti I Want to Know.* n.p.: WWOHD, 2012.

Frechette, Richard. *Haiti: The God of Tough Places, the Lord of Burnt Men.* New Brunswick: Transaction Publishers, 2012.

Garrigus, John D. *Before Haiti: Race and Citizenship in French Saint-Domingue*. New York: Palgrave Macmillan, 2011.

Goucher, Candice. *Congotay! Congotay! A Global History of Caribbean Food*. New York: Routledge, 2014.

Greene, Graham. *The Comedians*. New York: Penguin, 2005.

Hebblethwaite, B. "The Scapegoating of Haitian Vodou Religion: David Brooks's (2010) Claim That 'Voodoo' Is a 'Progress-Resistant' Cultural Influence." *Journal of Black Studies* 46 (1): 3–22, 2015.

Herskovits, Melville J. *Life in a Haitian Valley*. New York: Octagon, [1937] 1964.

Hurston, Zora Neale. *Tell My Horse: Voodoo and Life in Haiti and Jamaica*. New York: Amistad, 2008 (originally published 1938).

Lemoine, Patrick. *Fort Dimanche, Dungeon of Death*. Bloomington, IN: Trafford Publishing, 1999.

Magloire, Gérarde and Yelvington, Kevin A. "Haiti and the Anthropological Imagination: Jean-Price Mars, Melville J. Herskovitz, and Roger Bastide." *Gradhiva* 1: 127–152, 2005.

Marxsen, Patti M. *Tales from the Heart of Haiti*. Coconut Creek: Educa Vision, 2010.

Ortiz, Elisabeth Lambert. *The Complete Book of Caribbean Cooking*. Edison, NJ: Castle Books, 1995.

Phipps, Marilene. *The Company of Heaven: Stories from Haiti*. Iowa City: University of Iowa Press, 2010.

_____. *Crossroads and Unholy Water: Poems*. Carbondale: Southern Illinois University Press, 2000.

Price-Mars, Jean. *So Spoke the Uncle*. Trans. Magdaline W. Shannon. Washington, D.C.: Three Continents, [1928] 1983.

Renda, Mary A. *Taking Haiti: Military Occupation and the Culture of US. Imperialism, 1915-1940*. Chapel Hill: University of North Carolina Press, 2001.

Seabrook, William. *Magic Island*. New York: Harcourt & Brace, 1929.

Sepinwall, A. G. "Beyond *The Black Jacobins*: Haitian Revolutionary Historiography Comes of Age." *Journal of Haitian Studies* 23 (1): 4–34, 2017.

Tann, Mambo Chita. *Haitian Vodou: An Introduction to Haiti's Indigenous Spiritual Tradition*. Woodbury, MN: Llewellyn Publications, 2021.

Thomson, Ian. *Bon Jour Blanc: A Journey Through Haiti*. London: Vintage, 1992.

Turnbull, Wally R. *Hidden Meanings: Truth and Secret in Haiti's Creole Proverbs*. Durham, NC: Torchflame Books, 2019.

Valdman, Albert. *Haitian Creole-English-French Dictionary*. Bloomington: Indiana University Creole Institute, 1981.

Webb, Jack Daniel. *Haiti in the British Imagination: Imperial Worlds, 1847-1915*. Liverpool: Liverpool University Press, 2021.

Wolfe, Amy, compiler. *Mountain Maid Best Made Cookbook: A Complete Guide to Haitian Cooking ....* Port-au-Prince: Mountain Maid Self-Help Project, n.d.

Wolstein, Diane. *The Magic Orange Tree and Other Haitian Folktales*. New York: Schocken Books, 1997.

List of Illustrations

Acknowledgments

With every bit of writing I complete, to paraphrase Sir Isaac Newton, I still stand on many shoulders, those of the living, as well as the dead.

If they were alive today, I'd thank W. Somerset Maugham and Graham Greene for endless hours of enjoyable reading while I lived in Haiti and Africa. Their short stories still astound me with their profound and astute observations of human nature.

Superlative book-and-layout designer Cathy Gibbons Reedy deserves a standing ovation. Again, with *Mangoes & Roosters*, she created a work of art from my scribblings. Thank you!

Gary Allen, Janet Perlman, and Leo Racicot all deserve my heart-felt appreciation for reading the almost-final draft of *Mangoes & Roosters*. And being kind in their assessments!

In addition, I thank Wally Turnbull for his generosity in permitting me to quote the Haitian proverbs found in this book.

A word of gratitude also goes to all the writers in the Writers Alliance of Gainesville, especially Jessica Elliott.

And last, but never least, I thank Michael Bertelsen for standing by me through thick and thin.

About the Author

After years of living overseas, working with humanitarian aid projects in Paraguay, Honduras, Haiti, Morocco, and Burkina Faso, Cynthia D. Bertelsen now resides in Gainesville, Florida. There she writes and cooks and enjoys ice-free winters. Summers are another story. She is the author of *Mushroom: A Global History*; *"A Hastiness of Cooks": A Handbook for Deciphering Historic Recipes and Cookbooks*; *In the Shadow of Ravens: A Novel*; *Wisdom Soaked in Palm Oil: Journeying Through the Food and Flavors of Africa*; *Meatballs & Lefse: Memories and Recipes from a Scandinavian-American Farming Life*; *Stoves & Suitcases: Searching for Home in the World's Kitchens*; and *Take a Duck or a Goose: Eclectic Essays on English Cookery Through the Ages*. *"A Hastiness of Cooks"* won the Gourmand World Cookbook Awards in 2020 for Best in the World in Culinary History. *Meatballs & Lefse: Memories and Recipes from a Scandinavian-American Farming Life* placed as a Finalist in the 2021 Next Generation Indie Book Awards, longlisted for Memoir magazine's 2022 Book Awards, and won a 2022 President's silver medal from the Florida Authors and Publishers Association. *Stoves & Suitcases: Searching for Home in the World's Kitchens* won Best in the World in Food Writing from Gourmand World Cookbook Awards 2022 and a President's silver medal from the Florida Authors and Publishers Association 2022. She contributed numerous articles to various food encyclopedias, as well as dozens of book reviews. Her columns for the *Cedar Key Beacon* in Cedar Key, Florida, covered culinary history when few writers and academics paid attention to the subject. She holds a B.A. degree in Latin American Studies, an M.A in History, an M.S. in Human Nutrition and Foods, and an M.L.I.S in Library Science. Read more of her writing on her blog, "Cynthia D. Bertelsen: Gherkins & Tomatoes ... Since 2008," at cynthiadbertelsen.com.